Praise for Animal Husband

"Nancy Margulies is one of the most brilliant people I've ever encountered. And nowhere is her genius more obvious than in these stories. I would usually feel compelled to hate someone this talented, but for her I'm making an exception.

— Terri White Tate, author, performer, lecturer

"As writer, performer and educator my specialty is creating stories that push boundaries, exposing raw human experience, shining a light on that which is sometimes funny, sometimes touching, always entertaining. Nancy Margulies' work offers all that. I am amazed at the ease with which she consistently comes up with vignettes both from her vivid imagination and from her life.

Animal Husband is an excellent example of a talented writer willing to let anything bubble to the surface, revealing aspects of experience others might shy away from. I was mesmerized by the book. Each story presents a vivid context with a great economy of words; they are like poems, each with a perfect beginning-middle-end."

— Ann Randolph, playwright, performer

"Margulies' short stories inspired me to write. I purchased several as gifts for my family. Her rich words and characters come to life instantaneously and take us on a wild ride of the imagination, to places sometimes dark and deep. She investigates the kaleidoscope of human experience with its unexpected twists and turns. Her books always leave me wanting more!"

— Elizabeth Sale, Filmmaker, performer

Animal Husband

Written and Illustrated by:

Nancy Margulies

ISBN-13: 9781502899675

Mel C. Thompson Publishing Company

Parent label of:

Cyborg Productions
Blue Beetle Press
Citi-Voice Magazine

Mel C. Thompson Publishing Company
237 Kearny Street, # 102
San Francisco, CA
94108-4502, USA
(415) 596-3040
melvinbrand@yahoo.com
www.melcthompson.com

Acknowledgements

Thanks to:

My excellent editors, Kate Mayer
Mayer Ink: www.mayerink.com and
Joanne Ehrich: www.Zenjopress.com

Mel C. Thompson for his unique perspective
on life and his countless contributions to
the world of non-mainstream books

The Write Sisters who witnessed
the appearance of each of these stories and
provided endless amounts of encouragement.

My husband, Gary,
for his never-ending support.

Introduction

Meeting with fellow authors, I discovered the power of writing whatever comes to mind without judging or editing. One of us throws out a word or phrase as a "prompt," and for the next twelve minutes we write. What shows up for me every time is a short story that I usually complete as the twelve-minute buzzer sounds. It feels like taking dictation. I don't know in advance where the story is going or who is telling it. The characters who share their stories through me seem real. They are strangers, yet I feel compassion for their predicaments and gratitude for their honesty. Occasionally, the story that shows up is from my own life.

Animal Husband

by

Nancy Margulies

Mel C. Thompson Publishing Company
San Francisco, CA

Table of Contents

Chapter One: Someone's Childhood

What Doc Missed... 3
Lester... 5
What a Prince!.. 8
Papa's Crimes... 11
Frozen In Time.. 13
Better Half.. 15
Teacher Appreciation....................................... 17
Innocent Until... 20
Mighty Duo.. 22
Qué Es Esto?.. 25

Chapter Two: Insiders Out

Laugh and Shrug.. 29
Saved from Extinction...................................... 31
Left, Right?... 33
Roger the Snake... 35
Outhouse Blues.. 38
Miss Ollie's Crimes... 40
Ducks in a Row... 43
And the Winner Is... 45
Where's Tommy?... 47
You're Gonna Pay... 49

Chapter Three: Animal Husband

Outfit... 53
Scenes from a Past Incarnation........................ 55
Being Maggie.. 57
Room for a View... 60
Animal Husband.. 61
Handy, Man.. 64
Staying Positive.. 66
Impossible... 68
Too True.. 70

Chapter Four: True or False

Flying Down to Rio.. 75
Half Awake Dreaming... 77
Have a Seat... 79
True Story... 81
A Whiff of Fame.. 83
Thinking Too Much.. 85
The Mob.. 88
Birth of a Terrorist... 90
To Tell the Truth.. 92
True or False... 94
Not Me.. 96

Chapter Five: Sudden Friction

Dios Mio!... 99
Sorry, Honey... 101
Damn, Eugene... 102
She Laughed.. 104
Flying Hopes.. 106
Over Here..108
If Only.. 110
Best of All, Gloria...112

Chapter Six: Fine, You Win

Not in My Backyard... 117
The Plan... 119
Not One of Us.. 121
Sow You Shall Reap...122
Double-Crossed... 124
Oh, Adam... 127
Spare Room... 129
Blue Eyes.. 131
For Science.. 133
Alternative Ending.. 135

Chapter One
Someone's Childhood

What Doc Missed   prompt: Gift

Mama says I'm gifted. I picture me in a box covered with shiny foil paper, a big red bow on top. "See how he takes it all in?" she asks anyone who'll listen. Most people look at me kind of puzzled-like. "He's gifted," Mama explains, "clearly gifted, doesn't miss a thing."

It's true I do pay attention. I want to figure how other people can open their mouths and have words come out strung together to tell a story or ask for more potatoes, or say a dream they had.

I can open wide. I did it just this morning. The doc drove his little silver house-on-wheels onto the Res. I'd been waiting with Mama on the dusty road by the radio building, standing in line as the sun was coming up, hoping he was on time and didn't get the wrong day, which happens sometimes.

We were second after an old lady who wasn't sick but just likes the attention. Most of our people don't go for this doc, they like the old ways, taking herbs or being smoked to make them better.

But Mama isn't from here. She's just plain White with no ancestors back beyond her one grandma. She married in but never gave up her superstitions, favoring what she calls "real doctors."

The doc didn't look at Mama, only at me. "What seems to be the problem, you look fit as a fiddle." It wasn't exactly a question but Mamma answered saying how, gifted as I am, at six-years-old I still don't talk.

That's when the doc said, "Open up." I wondered if he'd see a lifetime of words stuck down there, maybe lined up neatly waiting their turn to be said. Then the doctor turned me around and banged on the metal wall making an awful racket. I jumped and turned to see what happened. The doc was smiling over my shoulder at no one in particular.

"Not deaf," he declared.

I looked to Mama. She seemed sad. I'm not the gift she wanted. I'm like something on Christmas morning that looks great, but when unwrapped turns out to be a too-big, ugly hand-knit sweater. The kind that gets bigger and dumber each time you wear it.

I wanted so bad to say something to make Mama smile. I opened my mouth and moved it around like people and dogs and even cats do, but nothing came out. So then I reached my arms around her legs and gave a hug. She looked down at me and smiled. "I hear you, honey, I love you, too."

Really, what more is there to say?

Lester   prompt: Chicken

In our house chicken is for Sundays. Period. Laundry is Wednesdays even on rainy days. Monday through Saturday girls do all manner of housework but never use tools from the shed. That's for boys. Ours is a house filled to the top with Dad's rules. Sunday chicken on the table means he decides which one, Bobby has to catch it, Billy chops off its head, me and mother pluck it clean, then she throws it in the pot with whatever's on hand.

Do some families eat chicken on Saturdays? I never thought to ask. Do some chickens deserve to die while others are meant for something greater? I didn't wonder 'til today when Aunt Margaret brought over two Rhode Island Reds and a passel of chicks.

"Keep 'em all, MaryLou," she told mother. "I can't have them cluckin' up a storm in town."

Aunt Margaret's farm was sold at auction, her livestock trucked up to Davenport. She's heading to Dell Haven where old people go when they got nothin' else. Mama cried, maybe over losing the farm she grew up on, maybe seeing how Margaret's ended old and broke after a lifetime of hard work.

I cried a little, too. I'm not sure why. Those baby chicks are so cute. The smallest one's bright yellow like the egg yoke he might've been. I've named him Lester in my mind, Les for short. Naming out loud is not permitted for any animal that might end up on our dinner table.

Secretly I hoped naming Les might save him from the hatchet. While Mama and Aunt Margaret sob away, patting each other's backs, I sneak Les up into my room to set him up in my old Hello Kitty lunchbox. There are already a few stickers on the inside, so it's like a pre-decorated room for him. I jab a few holes in the top with my school protractor and put him in his new home under my desk lamp to stay warm.

After lights out, with Les here, I can't sleep. I always spin in circles right before bed, spin til I am dizzy and might faint, then I throw myself on the bed and fall off to sleep. But tonight I'm still awake, listening for him, hoping he's happy, wishing I'd thought to feed him, making plans on how I'll make it up to him in the morning. I hear him rustlin' around in there. I'm wide awake when he first speaks to me. His voice is unusually deep for a little guy.

"SaraJean," he whispers, "are you awake?"

How could he know my name, I wonder. Besides, he isn't supposed to be able to talk. Before I can take all that in he says, "Sara Jean, move over and let me in. It's cold out here and you're so nice and warm."

I'm still wondering over his perfect English when he interrupts, "Dammit, Sara Jean, make room! You're not afraid of me are you?"

I manage a quiet reply, "No." My voice comes out squeaky, "Well, maybe," I tell him. "Maybe a little." I don't want to start out lying to my new pet on our first night together.

"Christ!" Les yells, sounding just like my dad when he's upset. "You're chicken, that's it!"

I'm shocked! How can this little pip-squeak chicken dare call *me* chicken?

The door to my bedroom slams hard. I peek out from under my blanket. Les's box is still where I left it. I decide he can just go to sleep without dinner and come morning I'll put him out with the others.

What nerve!

What a Prince!   prompt: Church

We live in the church, Papa, Mama and me. We eat there,
pray there, do our laundry there and when no one else is
around we worship the Devil there, too. Papa's in charge of
cleanliness for the whole church. Mama helps him, sews for
the ladies, bakes for Sunday socials. I worship the Devil on
my own time, Mama likes to say.

I'm not wild about the church or the people who come here.
But I am crazy for all things devilish. Down in the basement
near the Christmas decorations and broken saint statues we
keep our secret Lucifer Box. It's red, of course. Inside we
have chalices, freeze-dried blood offerings, a few dusty
animal parts, candles, matches, snack food in Tupperware
and several Devil worship sing-along books.

It's just the three of us since the Spencers passed. They
loved Lucifer like we do, but they were old and wore out. The
Devil has them now, Papa's fond of saying. We smile down
at the floor, imagining the Spencers dancing in flames with
their very own pitchforks.

Last week not much was happening among the Godly so we
had free time. Papa finished waxing the pews, Mama caught
up on mending and we headed down.

Now that I'm nine, I have responsibilities. I line up our
sacrilegious objects, making sure all is tidy. Mama turns off
the lights, leaving one small candle burning, then we chant
and conjure 'til the Devil himself comes right up through the
floor and stares us in the face with his red glowing eyes. He
never fails to appear. But last week he seemed different, not

as spooky or fierce. He sat down on the cold floor, let off a big fart of steam and put his head in his hands.

"Folks aren't going to Hell like they used to," he told Papa. "Sex and swearing and all manner of wildness have become acceptable. Sinning requires a lot of planning, and everyone is too busy playing Candy Crush or sexting their co-workers to go out and really lay down some Cardinal Sins."

He kind of shrank as he sat there; his red coloring faded to pink. He looked more like a Valentine cherub than the Prince of Darkness. I wanted to reach out and pat him on the back but I didn't want to singe my hand.

Mama, Papa and I sat down on the floor and put our heads down too, showing compassion and hoping that wouldn't offend the Devil.

"Can we help?" Papa asked.

"No, its hopeless," was the Devil's answer.

"Maybe we could murder the minister," Mama offered brightly.

"Thanks, that's sweet of you but no," he said. "I'm thinking of retiring."

"Papa looked shocked. "Retire and do what?" he asked. We all leaned in close to hear the answer.

"I'm thinking of consulting, maybe get into politics or corporate leadership — it's the last bastion of hope." The Devil seemed happier now. "And there's the Evangelicals, what the hell?" he grinned. "Lots of anger and judgment there, does my soul good. I'll finally have time to update my website on the DarkNet, too."

He was up now and dancing around, traces of smoke streaming out of his ears. We three let out a big sigh of relief, then tiptoed out, leaving the Devil to his details.

Papa's Crimes   prompt: Patient

"Be patient, Randolph, for God's sake." That's Mama. She loves to boss me. I hold my breath, taking up only 30 seconds. I recite most of the state capitols, look at the desert around our house, then run completely out of patience.

"Let's just go."

"Five more minutes."

"Two, *please*?"

We wait two minutes by Mama's calculation, then turn and walk back toward the mesa. Our home sits alone, an adobe one-room dark little place. Heading back is almost as discouraging as standing there waiting for Papa. He won't be here today, maybe not next week either. Promises mean nothing to this man but as Mama points out, we have to cut him some slack.

Papa *is* wanted in forty-three states for a total of twelve different crimes. They range from armed robbery to impersonating a rodeo star. Papa's full of imagination and not too fond of rules or laws. He's only broken four commandments: don't steal, kill, swear, and some other one, maybe more but four is all either of us can remember.

Waiting for Papa is a talent Mama perfected but not me, I am still trying to get my skills up. Today I have less than no patience because today, unlike the other no-show days, Papa promised to share his secrets: the Long Con, the Big Mitt, the Bank Boost and the Lady-Killer. That last one might be a way to get the gals, maybe, or it could be about murder.

I can't wait to find out which. But wait is what I've been doing all day. Wait and complain and now walk back home.

"Holy mask-of-Zorro," Mama yells.

I turn and see dust rising on the road behind us, then the bright orange jeep that is my father's comes into view and standing while somehow still steering, is my one-and-only Papa.

"Jump in Junior."

I jump.

"Farewell, my Lady!" This he says to mama with a tip of his bright blue ten-gallon hat and we're off.

This is it. This is my day, the one I've waited for my whole life.

"Son," Papa smiles down at me.

I nod eagerly.

"I retired last week. Age 50 means time to take it easy. We're moving to Miami. I have a condo in the Easy Lake Retirement Village. New ID for both of us. They allow kids your age as long as you keep quiet. We're stocked with TV dinners, soda and crossword puzzles. Just you and me, finally."

"And Mama?" I ask, feeling bad, watching her and the house shrink away in the rearview mirror. I have to wonder, what was her crime?

Frozen in Time   prompt 11/12/13

"...11-12-13..." me and the other guys count off. I end up unlucky 13, pretty much screwed from the start. It's only a game, supposedly, but it's more — 'cuz you can get hurt or killed or *worse* — known as chicken by everyone at school, all over Facebook, hell, all over the world.

When 12's turn comes up, knowing I'm next, I almost shit my pants. I'm like, how am I ever gonna make that last turn without going over the cliff? But 12 slams down the hill, board squealing, makes the final curve, flies halfway up the next hill then back pulls a fakie, rolls backward all the way to us. Beauty.

So now it's my turn. I switch stance, using my right foot to push, pop the board, grab it and run the rest of the way up to Bill, who's the Starting Mark. Before I even drop the board my whole life flashes in my eyes like they say happens before you die. Fourteen years go by in like a second or something. Birthday parties, scout camp, smoking reefer, spankings, school tests, recess, everything.

Then I'm on the board, flying down the hill, over to the half pipe easy, back on the hill, gaining speed, coming to the curve and then pop! Everything stops, I'm in the air, board still under me, guys all watching. I even notice a stray dog looking my way. Like we're all frozen in time, nothing moves. I count my breaths all the way up to 11, 12, 13 and then life starts back up, my body twisting, I leaned in, spin around, make the curve. Roll in to the guys who are all staring at me, eyes wide, jaws hanging.

"You saw?"

"Shit yes, we saw!"

"Was I like frozen in the air?"

"Dude, you were!"

So now the important part, "Who shot video?"

They all look at each other, phones in hands, shaking their heads.

Damn, I would have gone viral.

Better Half   prompt: Separation

Mrs. Jarvis separated Michael N and Jason for the third time today. It's Jason's fault. He talks too much, can't sit still and picks on girls. Michael just follows along. Michael is my twin although you wouldn't know it. For one thing he is sort of fat and for sure blond. I am skinny, which I hate, and my hair isn't any color. Just in between, just brownish.

We were one person when we were born. No, really. One. Our hips and our inside shoulders (my left, his right) were joined together so when he moved I had no choice. When we were little I didn't know we could move when *I* wanted. I always waited for him to move. Or wished we could move, and cried a little if we didn't, then he knew something was wrong and figured it out.

Most of the time Mom fed me. I liked that better than when she said, "Millicent, I know you can hold this spoon. Now do it." She'd put us in front of a mirror so I could see how Michael used his free hand to feed himself. I'd watch him hoping the food would fill my mouth as he spooned it into his. Eventually Mom would feed me with a frown on her face, making *tsk* sounds at me, then smiling over at Michael.

"You two are a rare breed," Dad used to tell us. Four-and-a-half was late for separating kids like us. There's always a risk one of us could die or suffer a stroke, the doctor told Mom right in front of us. But the surgery went fine and when I woke up I was in a giant hospital bed with a TV and a tray of food and the rest of me was across the room, feeding himself Jello.

I cried a little like usual but he didn't hear me. He grabbed the remote and turned on his TV. Mine remained dark. I tried moving my arm without any help from him or Mom or Dad. It moved a little. It hurt a lot.

No one asked me if I wanted the separation. It's been three years now. We aren't a rare breed any more, I guess. We are Michael who is friends with Jason and gets in trouble and I am "his-little-sister-who-is-so-quiet."

At night I dream us together again.

Teacher Appreciation   prompt: Alert

"There's a Nasty Bastard born every minute." Mama patted my head lovingly. "And remember, assholes come in all sizes, Lou Lou. Be alert."

I figure the other kindergarteners got different advice. Something about manners or making new friends.

I didn't need Mama's warning. I knew all about assholes, especially big ones like Daddy, Uncle Roy, all their buddies. "Nasty Bastards" is reserved for guys who do more than swear, spit, drink and holler. If a guy hits you or tries to get into your panties starting when you're still a kid, then he's a Nasty Bastard.

No one at my new school could shock or take me by surprise. Let 'em try.

Even so, I wasn't ready for Mrs. Nelson, my first-ever teacher. She lined us up on the playground, looked us over, then, taking her time she found something *nice* to say about each one of us, even if she had to make it up.

Take Tommy Wilkers, a scrawny kid who fidgets and mumbles and picks his nose.

"Tommy, or do you prefer Tom?" she asked, causing Tommy to act like a turtle, disappearing his head into his ratty t-shirt, then popping it out again.

"Tom," he mumbled.

"Tom, I can see you are a boy with lots of energy and many thoughts in your head," Ms. Nelson beamed in his direction. Tom wiped his nose on the back of his hand, nodded then stood up straight for once and grinned.

"And you, Lou Ellen," she leaned in close smelling like lemon and Sanka. "You're very grown up for your age. 'Mature' is the word."

Hell's bells, was she a mind reader, a witch or what? I could of kissed her on the spot but held my ground and just gave a little wink.

Mama made me report on my first day before Daddy got home and we had to shut up.

"Well?" Mama was waiting.

"It was OK. She said I'm mature." I tried to hide my pride. Pride is a sin, I know, and comes before a fall.

"Mature? What the Hell is that supposed to mean? You're five-years-old, or didn't she notice?"

"Maybe she meant like smart for my age or..."

Mama cut me off, "Girls mature at twelve or later. Don't let her tell you otherwise. That's all we need. Christ Almighty." Mama slapped her dishrag at a horsefly, sat down heavy and glared at me.

"Just go on up, Lou Lou, I got to get dinner fixed."

I went up to the closet where I keep my collection of assholes of all sizes. I spent all last summer collecting them. One used to be the little belly button from an orange, all cute and puckered up like a real baby asshole. The others are ends I cut off balloons. I've got plenty of the usual pink, blue, red and yellow.

But what some kids don't even know is there's purple balloons in this world, silver, sometimes, even black. And I've a gold shiny one. It's my best one, I call it "Champ." I didn't cut off the balloon part; I saved the whole thing.

Before the balloons I used to make a fist so my finger and thumb curved to look like an asshole. On the other side my pinky looked like a baby asshole. You can use these two built-in assholes if someone bigger acts mean. But don't let me catch you pulling that around Mrs. Nelson. She's better than that. She's a gold balloon in a world filled with assholes.

Innocent Until   prompt: Trouble

"Am I in trouble, Mom? Just tell me."

"I honestly don't know."

"Well, how did he sound?"

"Angry. Just go."

I tiptoe downstairs, pacing myself, imagining a spanking, wishing I was wearing my padded winter pants. Dad's waiting in his den — a study off the living room we are not allowed to enter. Being called in means only one thing.

"What's this?" He holds up a paper, waves it in my direction, throws it down, slamming his fist on the desk.

"I don't know — a note from my teacher?"

"Don't give me that innocent act, young lady."

"I really honestly don't know. Seriously, Dad."

"Seriously" is our code word for "I mean it." It's the word you use to get someone to stop tickling you if yelling "stop it" doesn't work. "Seriously" means I'm being one hundred percent honest. It always works.

"Don't give me that 'seriously' crap."

I'm stunned into silence.

"This is a police report," he yells. "This is a damned arson investigation, Rose, very incriminating findings."

My eyes well with tears. My own father thinks I'm capable of starting fires. How could he take their side and accuse me so easily? I shake my head.

"Dad" my voice is trembling, "Daddy, please. I'm only eleven. I'm your daughter. I would never ever start a fire. Where was this fire and how bad was it?" The words tumble out of my mouth before I can stop myself. I am curious after all.

Which fire has blazed out of control, I wonder? The church choir dressing room wastebasket? The trash bins behind Joe's pizza? Or was it the backseat of the old Pontiac in the Sears parking lot?

Dad seems to have forgotten me. He's leaning on both arms, examining the paper, muttering to himself.

"I'll give you the benefit of the doubt on this one, Missy."

I let out a sigh. "Dad, you're doing the right thing."

"Maybe. We'll see. Frankly I can't fathom a kid your age even getting into the ballpark at night."

My mind races back to June when I pulled that caper. There was nothing in the papers at the time. But, wow! I was more successful than I even dreamed. I walk around to Dad's side of the desk. "Scouts honor, Dad. I would never!"

"I know you wouldn't honey, but I had to ask."

"I forgive you, Dad."

Mighty Duo   prompt: Decision

Ma and me are The Mighty Duo. That's her name for us. I agree even if I don't know what a do-o is, exactly. Something like a do-over I think. I know "mighty" thanks to Mighty Mouse, a favorite of Ma and me. Mighty is a mouse from olden times. We have videos of him to watch over and over. He can fly, which most mouses can't. Good thing.

We are mighty and we are a do-o. Now that Daddy is gone who-knows-where, we are changing everything. Ma is doing-over the kitchen with new contact paper on the shelves. She got new dishcloths. She put carnations in the window. Cheering the place up, she calls it. But still she cries at dinner. She looks at the spot where Daddy's chair was. She pitched the chair out back. It's with the pick up on blocks and other junk.

"We don't need his crap," she reminds me.

"Yeah, who needs his crap?"

"Not us, son."

"Right, not us. Not now, not never."

We nod at each other, clink glasses, finish up our milk, clear the table. Time stretches long after dinner with no Daddy stomping around. No arguments, not even one plate thrown against a wall.

I stay up past bedtime. Ma doesn't notice. She tells me stories about how she met Daddy when she was just a girl. He was a friend of her Pa. He was a drummer. He could make anyone laugh. They called him Crazy Charlie. No one took him serious. Except Ma, that is. She looked up to him, him being older and all.

When Ma turned thirteen, Crazy Charlie whispered in her ear: "I am crazy for you!" Those words went right to her toes and made them tingle, she says. Her folks weren't paying any attention. They let Crazy Charlie spend time alone with Ma. When she turned up pregnant with me, they got to noticing fast.

Ma and Daddy got married quick in the next town over. A preacher there did the whole thing for free. He saved Ma's moral soul. Daddy moved in. When I was five we moved to our own place. Once he got Ma alone, Daddy acted different. Some nights he didn't come home. Other nights he showed up itching for a fight.

"Good riddance to bad rubbish," I tell her, thinking back on those nights.

"You said a mouthful there, sweetie."

We're taking our time with dinner dishes, saying the same things over and over. Ma's fixing to mop the floor when the front door opens and there he stands: Crazy Charlie, Daddy, Bad Rubbish.

My feet freeze in place but Ma moves fast across the room. She throws her arms around his neck like in the movies. She kisses his mouth.

"You and me, kid," Daddy grins down at her.

"The Mighty Duo," Ma answers, still hanging on him.

That's when my feet turn me around and head me out the back door. Ma and Daddy don't notice. I make a decision right then as I run across the field out back: I will keep running. I will live on my own. I'm almost seven, and big for my age. Like Mighty Mouse himself, I fly across the field and disappear into the night.

Qué Es Esto?   prompt: On the Other Side

My new Camp Lone Star friends want to know what's on the other side of this crazy-ass wall. I'm hanging back. Some mean guy might be waiting over there to hurt us bad.

Paying no attention to what I just said which was "No way m'gay!" They tell me "You go first," then shove me forward.

"No, morons." I whisper this in case someone over there is listening.

The wall is wire mostly but in front of us it's old, made of stone, covered with printed signs and graffiti about some girl named Patti who blows donkeys. I saw a glassblower once. He blew a bird. Maybe he taught this Patti Whoever.

The wall is way taller than us, stretching as far as we can see, stone then back to wire. We find a sign stuck under the wire printed in red: *Los Estados Unidos! No Entrada!* I figure the giant *"No"* means something like "Don't even think about it."

No entrada? Maybe *entrada* is a bad guy hiding out on the other side. *Los Estados Unidos* sounds like a gang name. While I try to figure out the sign Matt climbs the wall, Jimmy follows after. They land and start making chicken noises, throwing clods of dirt over, missing me by a mile.

"Come on chicken, what are you waiting for?" they say together, like they've practiced. I scramble up and over, fall the last part, end on my hands and knees looking at dirt, empty beer bottles, a baby rattle, something like a lady's red flower skirt, a child-sized guitar, all broken up.

It seems hotter over here, no trees, no shade, no nothin'. We want to start exploring, like the first men on the moon, looking for cool stuff to bring back, or signs of life, but we don't get a chance. These big guys with guns appear out of nowhere and look at us like we're the dumbest kids ever.

"You Gringo kids want to sneak *into* Mexico huh? Looking for jobs or your mama? You want to trade places?"

They switch over to Spanish, still laughing our way. Now seems like a really good time to climb back.

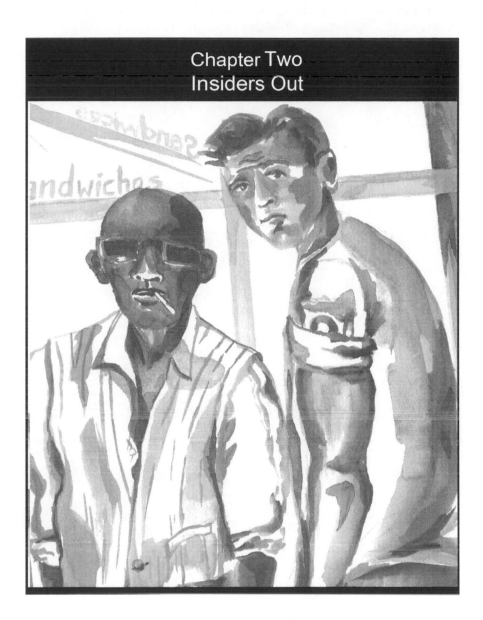

Chapter Two
Insiders Out

Laugh and Shrug   prompt: Bridge

Jim Creston threw his duffle over the side of bridge, didn't stay to watch it sink. The night before he'd left his genuine fur parka at some bar, grabbing a cheap windbreaker in its place. Dropping the duffle he let go of the last of his possessions: passport, dopp kit, orders to report at 0700 hours, all sinking, sinking, sunk.

The officer on duty didn't believe Creston. "Don't shit me, Sailor. Hand over the paperwork."

Creston just laughed and shrugged. He did a lot of that over the next few hours, laughing and shrugging at the Commanding Officer, the burly MPs, the Sheriff of San Diego County.

I doubt Creston planned this. He wasn't the type. He was a drinker, a party animal, a guy who let life happen to him while he sat back and watched or nodded off to sleep, drooling.

"What the hell do we do with this fuck?" The Lieutenant-Commander asked his Lieutenant. "We have zero paper work on him. Even the Sheriff can't hold him more than 48 hours. Think, man!"

No regulations covered Creston's actions. They had to let him go. He wandered off, penniless, into the blazing San Diego sun. One of the patrolmen said he heard Creston whistling. The guy had nerve.

It's anyone's guess what Creston did that day or the next. I didn't hear from him 'til ten years later. He called my home in St. Louis to relate the bridge story. I'm the one who'd dropped him off that morning. He'd told me to keep the Animal, his car, which was painted pink with black stripes.

After dropping him off, I'd driven the Animal home, went on to finish college, marry, have kids, in short: grow up.

Meanwhile Creston found the only work available for a guy with no documentation: maintenance crew on a cruise line. His charm, which was considerable when sober, and his good looks went a long way on board. He worked his way up to First Mate of the Ship Shape program, was later named Director of Senior Shufflers Meet-n-Greets. Then he disappeared. He probably had enough cash saved to buy reasonable ID. He had skills. His drinking was now moderate.

Creston was a new man. More than that, he possessed the names and addresses of some of the more prominent cruise line passengers. They all knew Creston, liked him. He married well, lived the good life.

Creston was at the height of his success the day he called me. He sounded sane and sober. I told him if he ever got to St. Louis he should look me up. I didn't mean it. He appeared on my doorstep the next day.

For old time's sake, and because it seemed important to him, I agreed to drive Creston to the bridge between St. Louis, Missouri and its much less wealthy counterpart, East St. Louis, Illinois. Creston jumped out of the car, suitcase in one hand, briefcase in the other and started across the bridge on foot. Just before he vanished from sight I saw him pitch the suitcase and briefcase over the rail. He turned, laughed, shrugged, and walked away.

Saved from Extinction   Prompt: Desperate

Danny was raised by wolves.

His mother, the lovely Naomi Lipshitz, was desperate to make her name in Hollywood. Danny's father, Mort Wolfe, was desperate, too, desperate to capture Naomi's heart. He felt bad about knocking her up but secretly hoped the child would lead to a lasting marriage. Naomi wanted no part of parenting or of Mort. Finding herself pregnant with Danny was inconvenient at best and didn't do her figure any favors, either.

The first pack of Wolfes to raise Danny were his dad's relatives. Grandma Wolfe took the boy for a year, then passed him off to a distant cousin in Africa, Sandy, who worked in a sanctuary in Algeria. She loved baby mammals, human and otherwise. She'd majored in wild life biology, and believed her True Life Purpose was saving the Algerian Grays from extinction.

Two years into a five-year commitment, Sandy knew with certainty that adorable cubs invariably grow aloof and menacing. She learned about Danny while skimming the Wolfe Family Annual Chanukah E-letter. Motivated by desperation and mounting loneliness, she signed lengthy guardianship papers and sent money to cover the expense of transporting Danny to Algeria,

Her story might have ended happily, if only Sandy had lived to see Danny arrive. Alone among a pack of Grays one winter afternoon, hoping to say her farewells before releasing them, Sandy was killed and devoured, hopefully in that order.

Danny arrived two days later. Placed in The Motherless Cubs Care Center, he was fed and cuddled as often as the young wolves and, like them, he thrived. Early on he picked up the cubs' growl-and-signal language and was eventually elected leader of the pack.

His human handlers never understood the power of the bond between Danny and his brothers until one fateful night. The chief handler may have attempted to remove Danny from the enclosure or maybe the door was left open. Danny and the cubs disappeared into the jungle. The handler's body was never recovered.

Years later, Danny Wolfe changed his name. He became Daniel G. Wolf, *The* Daniel G. Wolf, world-famous expert in pack behavior and a born leader. You may wish to hire him as a visiting lecturer for your Lions Club. He is an easy guest, preferring to sleep outdoors and requiring only one meal, daily. Just don't cross him.

Left, Right?   prompt: Grace

Grace Ann Meyers had two left feet. Not the metaphorical type, but two actual left feet. Both big toes on the right, two pairs of shoes required to make up one she could wear. As a baby she seemed normal enough, crawling and cooing right on schedule, but when it came time to walk little Grace was all thumbs. Not really, but you get the idea.

Grace was a sad choice of names, but how could her parents have known? Little Grace took many long minutes and several falls to traverse a room.

Taking the long route, clinging to walls, she did well enough. The whole town (all 728 of us) watched Grace with a mix of admiration and trepidation. What the hell would this kid do when it came time for school? She'd have to be excused from everything from Trick or Treating to the Senior Mixer. She could play a large-sized Baby Jesus in the school pageant. That was slim consolation.

Young Grace Ann fooled everyone. She invented her own dance forms: shuffles, jumps, glides and hops. She was given to wearing a toy drum around her neck, tapping out various beats to accompany her dance steps. Grace's sense of rhythm was excellent. Her attitude an admirable, "Can do!"

Over the years Grace became such a familiar sight, bopping around town, none of us thought much of it, until Rudy Hammersham came to town. A distant cousin of Mayor Jones, Rudy showed up for a family reunion — Rudy and his two right arms. It's not something you notice right off, left arm facing palm out, the odd way he grasped things, hugging them to his chest. He was introduced to Grace at the church social. They shook hands like any normal couple then took a longer look at one another. We held our collective breath, watching what we figured was a match made in heaven. Then Rudy turned away, Grace did the same. As if on cue they moved apart, him with a smooth glide, hands in pockets, she with a hop-jump-step.

Maybe those two thought of how their kids might turn out or how as a duo they'd always be known by their oddities. Rudy left town shortly thereafter. We never saw him again. Grace ended up moving to San Francisco where we heard she blended with all the lefties and felt right at home in Grace Cathedral.

Roger the Snake   prompt: Interview

Mr. Moskowitz ushered me into his grubby little office for the interview. The room looked like a former janitorial closet complete with the smell of Pine-Sol. Moskowitz, a small man, balding, dressed impeccably, was not at all what one would expect from a producer of soft porn.

"So, Miss Nipples, is that your real name?"

"No. Actually it is a stage name. I am Natalie Wood, the *other* Natalie Wood," I told him. I'm sick of that phrase but it's become automatic when sharing my true name. Miss Nipples is a nickname from high school but I didn't bother him with that.

"Miss Wood, tell me about your last *adventure*. I am looking for a time when you took a *big* risk."

My mind went into a spin, shooting out images of a multitude of less-than-careful life choices: the rock climbing, the hang gliding, the shop lifting, the public nudity, meals purchased from street vendors, that last high school reunion.

"My twentieth high school reunion," I blurted out.

Mr. Moskowitz looked disappointed. "That was risky?"

"It was, yes. Because I agreed to burst forth out of a cake dressed as a naughty nurse with a skirt short enough to show my snake tattoo."

Now I had his interest. "Snake tattoo, huh?"

"Yes, it's in honor of my longest relationship: with my pet boa, Roger."

"Wait, a snake named Roger? A relationship with a snake named Roger?"

I nodded. I smiled to show that the thought of Roger is a positive one.

"Is Roger available for an interview?" Moskowitz now leaned in, no longer appearing shy. He took off his glasses, smiled at me, and winked. "I would love to see the snake in our up-coming film."

I was thrilled, assuming this meant I would have a part in the next Pleasure Pit Production.

"You could have a role here," Moskowitz must have been reading my mind. "You can be the snake's agent. Negotiate, encourage, represent his interests."

"But what about me?" I asked. What about my nipples, I thought. He hadn't even asked to see them.

"You are a sweet young woman and I wish you well, but I am looking for an actor with authority, with a unique angle, with a link to original sin."

Original sin? I was all for sin, of course, but how original could one be in this day and age?

Moskowitz leaned across his cluttered desk. "Pleasure Pit Productions is a wholly owned subsidiary of the Church of Jesus the Savior," he explained. "Our films bring the bible to life. Perhaps you saw *When Cain was Able*. No? How about the blockbuster short subject, *David Does Goliath*? or *Thy*

Rod and Thy Super-Staff? No matter. For *Adam Had'em* I've cast a hot little Eve and the perfect Adam for scene one. I need your Roger to complete the ensemble. See if you can talk him in to coming in for an interview, I bet you're quite persuasive when you want to be. Here's a standard simple form contract... just in case."

With that he ended the interview and I went home to lick my wounds and convince my snake to sign on the dotted line.

Outhouse Blues   prompt: Identity

JoyLee Perkins lost her identity down an outhouse hole in
South Africa. Cape Town to be specific. A two-holer painted
the colors of liberation: red, yellow, green, black and blue.

JoyLee's husband, Ralph, was disgusted not only with the
smells wafting up from the sewage but with JoyLee for being
dumb enough to drop her entire travel pack into the muck.
Her passport, driver's license, credit card, the whole
shebang — floating briefly then sinking slowly out of sight.
The guide and other tourists looked none too pleased.

Ralph wanted to punch her out for ruining their vacation
before it even began but held his tongue, clenched his fists
and thrust them into his jacket pockets. "Too damned dumb,"
he mumbled so quietly only JoyLee heard. The other tourists
were already back in the van, peering through binoculars,
hoping to site a hippo or giraffe.

Standing over the stinky hole JoyLee seriously considered
lowering herself in. The opening wasn't wide enough, she
realized with great relief. Besides, who knows how deep that
pile of shit might be? Recovering her identity was out of the
question. Thank God for Ralph, she thought, he can vouch
for me, flash his American passport maybe a few twenties,
get the embassy to issue a new identity.

That's when it hit her: other than Ralph, no one in the entire
African continent knew who she was. Ralph, still mumbling,
shaking his head sadly side-to-side, was the only one who
could identify her. JoyLee took a long hard look at Ralph, her
husband of twenty-three years, still the same guy she'd
married, not a day more mature than he'd been at eighteen.

With shoulders hunched, hands deep in his pockets pulling down his green army jacket he looked like an unhappy toad.

JoyLee turned and began to walk quickly, then broke into a run, first on tiptoes, then with heels digging into the ground, pounding the dirt as she made her way away from the outhouse, away from Ralph. She didn't glance over her shoulder, didn't ask permission of the guide who'd driven them to the animal sanctuary. She ran. Her breath came hot and heavy, choking her at times, her heart pounded in her ears, still she ran.

A couple miles from Ralph she stopped, looked around and discovered she was a few yards from a highway. She briefly wondered if sticking her thumb out would mean hitchhiker in this foreign country. Thumb up, a slight hitch in her hips saying "pick me up, big boy" and she had to wait less than five minutes for a ride. A rust-covered pick-up, smelling vaguely like the outhouse, pulled over. The driver looked to be twenty at most, a smile on his face, he leaned across the front seat and opened the door for her. JoyLee climbed in and stared out the dusty windshield at the open road.

That's all we know of the former JoyLee Perkins. Ralph had a hard time describing her to the police. The embassy administrator asked about her moods, her dreams, the likelihood she would elect to disappear. Ralph was stumped. How did she feel? Her dreams? He drew a complete blank. With no photo of her and his internal image fading fast, Ralph was stymied. Her hair color? Brownish or something. Tan? Her eyes? Blue or green. No, more gray?

On the flight home Ralph held his wife's return ticket in his sweaty hand and stared at it — the only proof he had she'd ever existed. *And now*, he thought, *I guess I'll have to start my life over again, away from Whatshername.*

Miss Ollie's Crimes   prompt: Fire

It must have been autumn. I remember the smell of burning leaves. But that's not how our fire started. It was arson no matter how much Rosie's lawyer argued for accidental. Rosie worked for us, pretty much raised me and little Belle from our earliest memories right up to the week before the fire. She came from American Samoa. Her real name was Hia Lilli T. Ollie, a name I imagined yodeled over the Alps, echoing for miles. Dad gave her the name Rosie to help her fit in.

Before she came to work for us, Rosie murdered her husband on Christmas day, stabbing him once to the chest then calling for help. He was dead by the time the ambulance arrived. Rosie offered the EMTs slices of the pie that had started her domestic disturbance. They accepted. After a meal including turkey and homemade cranberry sauce the men took Rosie's husband away leaving her to mop up the blood.

We knew none of this when Rosie first came to work for us. Dad is a lawyer, a firm believer in the letter of the law. Anyone found innocent is, therefore, innocent, including Rosie. I wonder if Dad renamed her to keep people from recognizing Hia Lilli Ollie and wondering why she was trusted with two young children.

Even Mama didn't know Rosie's past 'til the night Judge Bannon came to dinner. The judge is a friend of Dad's and the first African American to preside over any court in Nebraska. Rosie's duties included donning a white uniform for company. On the night the judge was among our guests Rosie walked in with a platter of food.

The Judge said, "Evenin' Miss Ollie."

She replied, "Evenin' Judge."

I wondered how they knew each other. Mama must have wondered, too. That night I heard Dad yelling at Mama, "Anyone found not guilty by a jury of twelve is therefore innocent, dammit."

Mama backed down that night but she talked to the Judge's wife soon after and learned of Rosie's guilt. She had a slick lawyer who played on the jury's sympathy, recreating the scene in which poor Miz Ollie made a lovely turkey dinner complete with cherry pie for dessert. Her ungrateful drunken husband complained about the pie — he wanted apple. For emphasis, he threw the gravy boat at her. In a moment of Christmas insanity Rosie went after him with her turkey-slicing knife. Judge Bannon was new to the District Attorney's office. A more seasoned prosecutor would have gotten her life.

Rosie murdered only once, was technically not guilty and we adored her. She was kind to us kids, cooked like no one we knew and sang gospel hymns that made our house feel holy. The first year with Rosie was the best of my childhood. But then she took up drinking again and turned mean. Some nights I could hear her banging around in the kitchen long after lights out. One night Mama and Dad came in late from a party and found Rosie on the couch drunk and ready for a fight. Dad didn't raise his voice; he just shushed her off to bed. The next morning he fired her.

When little Belle heard about the firing, she pictured Rosie up in flames or melting like the Wicked Witch of the West. I told her not to worry, being fired had nothing to do with fire. But I was wrong.

Rosie didn't want to hurt us so she started the fire while we were up at the lake. When we returned to the house, almost all of it was gone, nothing but smoldering ashes with a stone chimney standing alone in the midst of it.

And all around us the smell of leaves that had burned up along with the house. Yes, it was autumn, I'm sure. Little Belle cried and said she wished we'd had a fire escape. There's no escaping some things I told her. Life's like that.

Ducks in a Row   prompt: Mistake

Like I told my wife, what happened back in April was a mistake. Nothing intentional, obviously. I mean who would want to run over a whole school of baby ducks? Or a flock, or whatever they're called. My truck isn't reliable, the brakes gave way, I was distracted, take your pick. I don't have an excuse handy. Besides, running over those little quackers was only the beginning. I have to give myself some credit here: I did stop, pulling over on the muddy shoulder of Highway 12. I examined the corpses but no need to dwell on that. They were squashed flatter than Mom's pancakes.

I was standing there shaking my head when something flew into my face, talons first, and dug into my cheeks. I screamed and beat at it but the damned thing held on. That's when the SUV must of come barreling over the crest of the hill and hit my truck from the back. The bird that had blinded me flew off leaving me bloody and crazed. The SUV was full of a bunch of town toughs. They jumped out of their vehicle and ran over to me as if I'd done something wrong.

"I'm the injured party here," I told them, "and remember, this duck thing was a mistake."

But those guys saw it different. They told me I had to pay for the damage to their bumper.

"Who ran into who?" I asked.

Their answer: a kick to my shins, a punch to my gut and a whole series of blows that came on so fast I lost track. I woke up in some makeshift hospital the army set up for the training camp just outside of town. I guess the soldiers came upon me there on the highway and figured I'd stopped to rescue the ducks, then been sideswiped by a hit and run. Thought they had it all worked out. Their mistake, my good fortune. I was treated for my busted ribs and cut up face, fed real good and told I was a hero. I guess they were short on real bravery, there being no war to speak of that particular year.

The local papers were called and my wife notified. When I felt better the Shriners threw a pancake celebration breakfast for me. The grandkids came. My wife and even my Ex showed up. Somebody made up T-shirts with little duckies crossing the road and my name in a heart above them where the sun should be.

It was a mistake, but there was no use trying to sort it out at that point. My truck got fixed up real good by the local mechanics union fellows — no charge — and I was offered a job at the Humane Society, the first steady work I've had in years.

I got no complaints.

And the Winner Is...   prompt: Collage

Ripping a photo from the album, tearing the head off my college boyfriend, balancing it on a pine tree like a christmas angel, I complete my first collage. Immediately I start a new one using a Safeway flyer: frozen pot roasts, four-packs of Wonder Bread, iced tea mix. This collage, "Food for Thought," doesn't look right 'til I add the head and arms of my mother at age twenty-one. I ripped her apart wishing I could have managed such a feat in real life, destroying her before she had a chance to meet my father.

Then the OT Lady comes around to my table and stands looming over me: "Francie, you don't want to destroy your photo album, do you?"

Odd question, obviously I do. There are only a few photos left, the others lay in tatters on the table where spilled Elmer's threatens to hold them in place for all eternity. I don't bother to answer her.

"Francie?" she bends over, her face inches from mine, her minty breath sickly sweet.

I grab one of the remaining photos and stuff it in my mouth. Now the smell of mint is replaced by a chemical taste, not at all unpleasant.

"Alright everyone," the OT turns her attention to the scattering of mental patients each hard at work on their assigned Family Collage, "Time's almost up. Let's clean our workspace and hand in your art. I will post the winner in the dayroom for all to enjoy."

Winner? Was this woman more nuts than the rest of us? Winner? What exactly are the rules of this competition? Maybe its ten points for the most horrific childhood, ten points for the earliest trauma, ten more if you tear up your collage and refuse to reassemble it.

I grab what's left of the photo of my maternal grandmother, dip it in a puddle of glue and slap it onto my arm. Good old Grandma Jean. She visited Mom in the hospital within a few hours of my birth, picked me up and said, "Rayleen, I want you to give this baby to me. Joe wants a baby real bad and I can't seem to get pregnant. You're young. You can always have more. I want this one, this girl."

Mom refused at first, or so she claims, but after a few sleepless nights back home with me, she relented. Grandma Jean kept me for almost two years. At that point I was hell on wheels according to her. Mom had moved away to Omaha, so Grandma dropped me off at the firehouse.

That's my story. It should be enough to make *me* The Fucked-Up Family Collage Winner and Champion.

Where's Tommy?   prompt: Misfit

Tommy Langdon never once fit in. His first few days in
Methodist Hospital were a disaster. The other newborns
cried if he was placed near them, nurses hesitated to pick
him up. It might have been the greenish cast to his skin, or
the fact that he had a mop of hair, two pointed teeth in front
and an odd way of grinning at people.

His mother loved him on sight, but she remained alone in
that sentiment. The father was listed as unknown, but the
truth is he's the infamous Billy "Knuckles" Langdon, another
misfit, a drifter.

At ten, Tommy began lurking around the bus depot, spraying
buildings with images of over-sized muskrats with lightbulbs
in their mouths. Attempts to punish or deter him only led to
more art in new locations featuring new animals. As fast as
the walls were cleaned they filled with grafitti. The town
psychologist recommended ignoring Tommy's anti-social
behavior.

"Pay no attention," she advised the mayor. "Stop cleaning up
after him. Leave the art be and he'll grow bored of it."

With no one erasing his art, Tommy went into overtime
production mode. He painted purple sardines and golden
lightbulbs along the base of the town's statue. He then
expanded his repertoire to include an entire ocean scene,
complete with an embracing octopus and whale covering
the east wall of the only church in town.

The next night, he added images of Adam and Eve,
complete with an inviting apple tree dripping with fruit. Still,

the town ignored Tommy publicly; in private, they began to mutter about him using descriptors like "talented" and even "genius".

Outsiders began to take notice, snapping photos of the wall with their phones, posting God knows where.

One crisp October morning, the mayor knocked on the rusty shed door where Tommy was reported to live. Tommy answered eventually. He'd been awakened, of course, being a nocturnal sort, and was not pleased with the racket, grumbled about needing his sleep. What transpired next is anyone's guess.

According to the mayor all went well. Tommy appeared pleased with the accolades and said he would consider a commission to complete the mural. He seemed surprised to learn about visitors from out of town, even from neighboring states, driving miles to witness his public art displays. That's what the mayor claims, but one has to wonder. The painting stopped as of that very day. Not one new image appeared.

Tommy is rumored to have moved to Manhattan, although he was also sighted in Boise, Dayton and as far west as Omaha. Although most townsfolk are disappointed, I don't really blame Tommy for moving on. There's nothing worse for a confirmed misfit than public acclaim.

You're Gonna Pay   prompt: Orange

Oranges everywhere, smashed into paving stones, rolling down gutters, under horse's hooves. Sammy the Slammer didn't mean it. He was running from the cops and the cart was in his way; suddenly oranges everywhere caused him to fall, face-first onto the bricks. His nose gushed blood, he lost a tooth, his palms were scraped raw on what promised be the worst day of his young life.

The cops stopped blowing their whistles, caught their balance. One of them grabbed Sammy by the forearm.

"You're gonna pay for them oranges, kid, and that's just for starters."

The precinct was four blocks away. Sammy'd lost a shoe in the fall; he limped along, one hand to his profusely bleeding nose, the other across his middle holding fast to the real reason he was running: a freshly-stolen lady's two-carat diamond ring, nestled neatly in his navel.

There were no beds free in Juvie. Sammy ended up in holding with four drunks and a crazy-looking homeless guy named Reefe. With no place to lie down or clean a wound, Sammy hobbled to the one free corner and slid to the floor. He intended to stay alert, keep his eyes on Reefe, but exhaustion and loss of blood had other plans for him. When he awoke, it was just him and Reefe. No longer in the cell, they were under a stinky tarp in the back of a cart. The wood planks of the cart reeked of rotten oranges, but Sammy smelled only dried blood. Reefe, on the other hand, his face pressed to the boards, inhaled deeply.

"I got you out, kid. You can thank me later. We're heading south, far south to where you can pick oranges right off trees, get paid for doin' it, kid. Ever been paid for doin' it?"

Sammy'd been paid for running all manner of errands, for breaking a host of rules and regulations, for hitting guys or grabbing purses, but never for something legit. The diamond was still lodged in his belly button, the night air was cool, the tarp provided good cover; the road smooth enough so his nose stopped hurting. Sammy pushed the tarp aside and looked up at the inky sky with its harvest moon, big and orange. That's the moment when Sammy's worst day became his best. Right then.

Chapter Three
Animal Husband

Outfit   prompt: Adventure

I'm a reasonable guy, but she called my uniform an 'outfit' for God's sake: "I like your outfit, Russell," LoriJean let me know and I'm supposed to say *thanks*? LoriJean is typical of the girls around home.

True, I joined the Navy partly because I like how sailors look, the ones on leave in San Diego, in old-time movies. Plus I joined because there's nothing to do around home except hang out with guys I've known since forever and try to pick up chicks — the same ones I've been trying to score with since junior high. I figured a uniform would get me the hell out and maybe land me some farewell-sailor-action, too.

The recruiter in Lincoln promised job training, quick advancement and adventure. Plus he said I'd be protecting America's freedom.

"After all freedom isn't free," he tells me. I never thought of that before, but it seems true enough.

In my new "outfit", Dad's Army duffel stuffed in the overhead, seated next to an old colored guy, I'm on a bus heading to Missouri.

An hour outside Omaha, the driver lets us out to stretch and buy snack food. That's where I see this super pretty blonde about sixteen or so, working the cash register. I get my Twinkies and am heading back to the bus when she calls out, "I love a man in uniform." That turns my head and hits me smack in the heart. I know her words aren't original, but I love the way she says 'em. I hurry to the bus, grab my duffel and run back into the Quik Mart.

Turns out her name is Tawnie, she's seventeen, employed, with an apartment all her own out back of the station. That's all it takes. I go AWOL before I've even seen a ship.

Us two all cozy up in her bedroom is all the adventure I need. I have to protect *my* freedom first. The rest can come later, right?

Scenes from a Past Incarnation   prompt: Escape

Our fire escape, never once used to escape a fire, was a source of joy summers, north of Hamburg. My brother in that past lifetime, I don't recall his name, ran with me zig zag up and down those wooden stairs, pursued by imaginary ghosts, peering into windows of off-limits rooms. The fire escape was our playground.

We couldn't wait for summer, when summer maids pulled white sheets off furniture with a snap. Heavy wooden shutters latched open revealing expansive, roiling waters of the North Sea. Playing on the fire escape is all I recall of my childhood in that incarnation.

My other memory from that lifetime takes place decades later. I'm now a doctor, and I'm filled with remorse. The wooden stairs no longer beckon to me. Next week, I will sail to Britain. Standing in our summer home in front of an upstairs window, I reach to close the shutters, then hesitate.

I'm determined not to forget my shame and its link to this house: dozens of women, children, the occasional man, all Jews, every one of them died here. My makeshift clinic couldn't provide the medicine, the supplies, the staff to care for them. I prolonged their lives, but in the end their wounds were more than I could heal with good intentions. I take a breath and vow: I will never forget this moment.

The fire escape memory and that one last remorseful scene, are all that remain of my past lifetime in Germany. Yet, most nights in my present life I dream myself back to the seaside house. Last spring, my husband and I traveled to Germany for him to deliver a lecture in Hamburg. While we were so far north, we searched for the house of my dreams; the house of my past lifetime.

Amazed, we found it. From the front it was just as remembered. The current owner showed us around. When she led us to the back, I was stunned. The fire escape was reduced to a ghost landing, only one charred step remained. I felt its loss like a blow to the chest.

"Are you alright dear?"

"Yes, it's just the stairs, all those stairs and the fire escape." I stammer.

"Lost to a fire. Burned down without harming the house. A miracle of sorts," she seems pleased. "Rumor has it the doctor who lived here was harboring Jews. The Nazis may have started the fire. No bodies were found, I guess she'd already run off, the doctor. We'll never know."

Being Maggie   prompt: Green

Green with envy. Green with seasickness. Green, as in unschooled, lacking experience. I've been green in all three senses of the word, simultaneously.

Back in high school, I wanted to be like Maggie Michaelson. Actually, I wanted to *be* Maggie. She was leader of the most popular girls. She had an older boyfriend. She had breasts that were just right, not too small like mine, not too big like Roseanne's whom boys taunted mercilessly, making moo sounds when she walked by. Maggie commanded too much respect for anyone to dare tease her.

Maggie's older boyfriend owned a boat, more accurately, he regularly stole the keys to his father's boat. The Des Moines river is narrow, muddy and only known to people living in Iowa. No one else would bother. I felt lucky to be included and desperate to fit in, so I drank my first beer — the ultra-cool Coors — which I chugged. Then I chugged another. I promptly threw up into the wind, drenching Maggie and her boyfriend. They dropped me at the dock. I walked home, wet and miserable.

After we graduated, while most of us stayed in Des Moines, Maggie moved to Manhattan, naturally.

Years later, visiting New York, I decided to get in touch with Maggie. I heard she lived in The Village. I heard she was an artist. How unbelievably cool. I prepared to envy her all the more.

Maggie's apartment was nothing to inspire jealousy. It was tiny and creepy. She apparently collected used chewing gum. One wall was a mural of sorts made entirely of gum and wrappers. She collected lint from the laundromat, thick gray gobs of it, which she affixed to another wall. The lint mural faced the gum mural. In between were mattresses, all once discarded, now claimed by Maggie and repurposed as her "Guest Room". They were graffitied with various names and cartoon images.

"Its my commentary on our throw-away world," she told me, "the gummed up sidewalks, piles of trash, the useless stuff we create."

She handed me a giant black marker. "Pick out a crash pad. Write your name on it, and you're home free."

Maggie plopped down on her own mattress, offered me a stick of Doublemint. I accepted, and sat down gingerly on the edge of an almost-clean mattress.

"What was real for you in high school?" I *think* that's what Maggie asked. With both of us chomping on our wads of gum, she was hard to understand.

"What was real?" I thought back to my humiliation, envy, desire to be someone else, my father, his rages, my mother, her passivity. What else was true about high school? How much should I reveal?

"You first," I blurted out, sounding like I was back in high school.

"OK," Maggie was game. She spit her gum into her hand, leaned toward me. "My father was 'real' — real mean, real scary, real sick. He got mad at me one night and ripped the curlers from my hair. My scalp was bleeding all over. I had to stay home for a week. He hit us whenever he thought we'd done something wrong. Most of the time he imagined it, and Mom never stood up to him. I was miserable in high school."

Maggie miserable? Maggie frightened? Suddenly the icon of popularity was my kin. A flood of memories washed over me, washed clean the room, its sticky walls, filthy mattresses. I saw my father, his incredible cruelty, my fear of him. I told Maggie about crying myself to sleep night after night, needing to get up extra early to give my eyes a chance to become less red and puffy. She nodded knowingly.

"Did your Dad ever ... you know?" Peggy asked.

I pretended I didn't know. I let her go first again.

"My Dad crawled into my bed. I pretended to be asleep," she confessed.

"Me, too," was all I could say.

I left there amazed by Maggie 's bravery and honesty and jealous all over again.

Room for a View   prompt: Moon

I was driving with my daughter yesterday,
backing out of a parking space. I said to her,

"Damn, there is a giant blue van behind me. I can't see
around it at all."

I peered into the rearview mirror. I honked my horn.
I looked over my shoulder then and said to her,

"Oh never mind. It's the sky."

A brilliant blue.

Living on the coast on a promontory near the light house
surrounded by fog for weeks on end I'd forgotten how blue
the sky could be.

And last night, that same clear sky allowed the moon
to brighten our bedroom, pouring its blue-white
through the windows, bouncing off mirrors.

I awoke and considered dancing about in a diaphanous
gown as an ode to the moon but opted to put a pillow over
my head and go back to sleep.

Animal Husband   prompt: Notice

His wife, Amanda, was the first to notice. It figures. They
lived together, worked all day side by side. Strange, she
didn't tell anyone. Seems she didn't feel the need to reach
out for help, research it on the Internet, do something.
Instead she tucked the whole thing away in some far corner
of her brain and went on with life as always. If she'd
approached me, it might have gone like this:

"Ray, I am concerned about Bill. He is acting strange."

"Bill? He's always been so, well, normal." At that point I'd
probably think the word dull applied best but would keep that
to myself.

"He *was* normal," Amanda would agree, "but now he makes
animal sounds. Cows, ducks, crows. He does a great
hummingbird you have to listen closely to even hear."

"Does he, ah, make these sounds for the grandkids or
something?"

"No, no, it's not like that. He makes them while we're pruning
in the orchard or canning, any old time. He starts in with the
sounds; goes on for hours. I'm used to that by now, but what
bothers me is he doesn't walk upright any more."

"Pardon me?" I might ask, buying myself time to take this all
in. I would picture Bill, tall and lanky, well into his '70s
crawling abound like a baby. "Like a baby?" I'd inquire.

"Jesus, no, Ray. Not like that at all. It depends, like a cow,
like a wolf. He does a great cat stretch. He can move like an

eel, too, but only on the linoleum. On the shag in the TV room he does a beetle, I think. Or it could be a cockroach, but I hate to think of having those critters in the house."

That's the conversation we never had. Amanda kept the revelations to herself. Only when I found her ledger book, did I learn about Bill's animal impersonations. She'd given up keeping track of bushels harvested and orders of mason jars received and began to sketch the animals, always labeling them Bill with a last name of Cow, Duck, etc. There were some diary-type entries that showed her concern with phrases like, "my husband, always so sweet, now an animal."

If Rita had reached out, we could have taken Bill in for testing or found him a nice pasture to graze. Maybe the vet, Doc Hadley, would have come up with a diagnosis, given him some Terramycin, which will heal just about anything in livestock.

Instead, unchecked, Bill continued to morph. One day he would be right as rain — I saw him on those days, market days for example and he was fine. Next day, alone with Amanda, he might pose as a lamp post for hours on end.

Amanda was handy with colored pencils, so she sketched him with his hands at his sides, lampshade on his head bright glow about his face. Next, if I read her notes right, he preferred to eat off a plate on the floor, then off the floor directly.

She gave up when he refused to be housebroken and penned him in the back, out past the old barn.

Last week, they took the both of them off. He's staying with his sister over by Chesterton. They tell me Amanda's in

Mount Mercy Psychiatric for observation, of all things. I can't imagine why they'd blame her for keeping all that to herself.

Handy, Man   prompt: Repair

I drive my beat up truck a mile or more to this rich lady's
house. I see fountains, naked statues, a bunch of flowers
and grass almost as perfect as Astroturf. There's no cars in
sight, but then I spy a garage with four doors. Jesus.

I park in front, start to honk the horn to let 'em know I'm here
but think better of it. The door is way too big unless giants
live here. At eye level is a big old lion's head — looks to be
gold. I give it a tug to see if maybe I could pocket it on my
way out, but it's on there solid. Me pulling on it must of rang
a bell inside. I hear it faint-like then foot steps. A guy dressed
up like for a wedding or funeral opens the door, looks me
over, making me feel like bubble gum he just scraped off his
shoe, then he says, "Yes?" in a phony British accent. I've
seen enough Beatles movies to know what Brits are
supposed to sound like.

"I'm the repair guy," I tell him.

He says nothing, holds up one finger to me and walks back
in the house. I quick step inside, take a look around.
When Mr. Silent Treatment comes back he motions to me to
follow him. We walk up a staircase like Gone with the Wind
and into a giant room with a four-poster bed big enough for a
whole scout troop to camp out on.

When I get closer I see there's a woman in the bed, under all
these shiny covers, head on a heap of pillows. I put down my
tool kit, step in for a closer look. She's a youngish model,
maybe twenty or so, could be quite pretty, but right now you
can't tell. Her face is all rearranged. I've seen worse but
she's right up there: two eyes on one side, mouth almost

sideways, nice nose, pretty much where it belongs, ears missing all together.

"OK," I turn to Mr. Snooty, "I'll take it from here. Leave us alone."

I lose track of time and when I look up from my repair work it's pitch dark outside. I turn on the bedside lamp and bring a mirror out of my kit.

"What do you think?" I ask her.

"Amazing!" I think she says. Her mouth is probably a bit stiff after being restored.

She manages a great smile. Her eyes, now placed above her nose, one on each side, well up with tears of thanks. With all the excitement, we both forgot the ears but I figure she can print up a couple new ones on her 3D. They come with instructions anyone can follow.

Before I leave, I reboot her and run a backup to iCloud 4.2 I think of asking her out for a beer, or whatever rich people drink, but I don't like to mix with girlbots. They're always breaking down. Call me old fashioned, I like to date carbon-based life forms. They're self-repairing.

Staying Positive   prompt: Preparedness Kit

Long ago, I packed batteries, blankets, the usual stuff, kept it by the front door in a giant tupperware chest. Jackets, scarves, cans of tuna. I was prepared. But when the big one hit, I wasn't home. I was up the block at the Krasnee's playing bridge like I do every Saturday.

Out of nowhere, the walls shake. Paintings crash to the ground, expelling daggers of glass. The ceiling falls in chunks, one slamming down on the card table sending plaster and clouds of dust in all directions. Bill and Martha head for the kitchen. Moments later, something big and heavy crushes that end of the house. I dare not look.

Limping home along the upturned sidewalk, I feel hopeful my house has been spared. I plan to open the bin, pull out the tuna and picnic in my yard, watch panicked neighbors run back and forth, listen for ambulances, that sort of thing. All this puts me in a pretty good mood, the Krasnee's fate forgotten, as I mentally run through my kit wondering if there's any chocolate in there.

When I turn the corner onto my street, I almost fall headfirst into a massive cavern that used to be the Riley's house. I catch myself right on the brink, stagger back a step, peer down into a tangle of cables, sewer pipes, scurrying rats: the stuff of nightmares.

Stay positive, I tell myself. It's then I notice the absence of my house. It's no longer where it belongs, second from the corner. In its place is yet another gaping hole. I walk slowly toward the edge, look down and there's my roof, not a shingle missing, the chimney is toppled but, other than that, things look in fine order. The sides of the cavern are sloped so I inched my way down. The living room window is open, rather the glass is missing, so I carefully climb in. In no time flat I locate my preparedness kit and pop the lid. I set up the giant flashlight, crank up the radio, open a can of water chestnuts and compliment myself on my ability to plan ahead.

Impossible   prompt: Beach

Marsha lost track of time. She'd been walking for hours, following the footsteps of some unknown person, probably a man. He would be barefoot, of course, wearing faded shorts, lean legs. She imagined him to be a vagabond, long haired, shirtless, tan, walking with no purpose, eyes cast down watching for sharp shell fragments.

She placed her small foot carefully into his large print then looked for the next footprint. In that moment, she witnessed the impossible: the trail ended beneath her. Frozen in place, mid-step, she stared at the smooth, unbroken expanse of compact beach stretching back toward the highway. The unknown person she was following had vanished.

"Impossible," she muttered to herself, "Impossible."

After studying the beach in all directions, seeing no signs of him, Marsha looked down at her own foot. It now filled the footprint perfectly. Her leg looked so tan in this light, the dark hair on it almost the same hue — wait! She'd shaved her legs that morning, and never had they been that hairy. Never. She studied her hands which were oddly big and strong, veined. Her white shorts were now baggy, faded khaki. Staring in disbelief at her flat chest, Marsha ran her rough hands over the hair that grew there. Tentatively she touched her face, discovering a mustache and a stubble of beard.

Marsha let out a loud, boisterous, deep laugh. "What the fuck, man?" She heard herself say.

Then, shaking his head side to side, glancing around to be sure no one had witnessed his strange transformation, Marshall, continued his walk. One step in front of the other. No hurry, no appointments to keep, ample time for a beach stroll. Later he would set up his sleeping bag for the night. Funny, he thought, how the mind plays tricks. It seems as if moments ago I was someone else, a young woman walking in white shorts, stepping into a man's footprints in the sand...

Too True   prompt: Messenger

Don't kill the messenger. The messenger in the case of Dad
was Mom. She called to say he was dead, lied about how it
happened, and later told the truth: it was suicide. He wanted
out.

The messenger with my sister, Ann, was Mom again. This
time on the phone. I jumped on a plane, cried the whole way
to Iowa. Mom met me at the airport and told me the truth.
It was suicide.

The messenger with Ellen was my brother Tom. He called
one Saturday afternoon and asked to come over. He'd never
done that before. When he showed up he wanted us to go
for a walk, another first. A block into the walk he told me: It
was murder and suicide. Ellen's husband shot her then
himself.

The messengers show up more frequently now, friends email
telling of their parent's deaths, reunion committees announce
the classmates who won't be attending future gatherings.
Phone calls, cards, hospital personnel. Death by cancer, car
wreck, old age, causes unknown.

When the phone rings late at night I am sure it's another
messenger. If the door bell rings when no one is expected
my heart pounds as I imagine a couple of World War II
soldiers prepared to deliver bad news.

When Grandmother Julia learned of my sister Ann's death,
she just sighed and said, "Another one gone." She was like
that when any of her friends passed away. She was used to
loss. My mother is used to loss, doesn't let those suicides

and other unexpected deaths get in the way of her pleasant life. Maybe I could be more like Mom and Grandma and roll with loss. Maybe. But that's not what I want. I want to fear the loss.

I want to kill the messenger.

Chapter Four
True or False

Flying Down to Rio   prompt: Flying

Mac had owned his pilot's license for all of two months when he decided fly to Rio. This isn't permitted, technically, but Mac's buddy Randy agreed to sign on as pilot when they filed flight plans.

As Captain of his own ship Mac was in heaven. The sky was bright, the winds nonexistent and Randy the perfect companion: fast asleep as soon as they were air-born.

The lovely ladies of Rio decked out in elaborate headgear, ruffled skirts with slits up the front danced in Mac's imagination as he anticipated his first night in the city of his dreams. His knowledge of Rio was limited to Fred and Ginger circa 1933 overlaid with the animated "Rio" in which Angry Birds fearlessly dive-bomb gibbering monkeys.

Mac pictured himself, a beauty on each arm, unseen castanets beating, strolling through a white marble casino lobby. Animated birds a la Uncle Remus' "Zip-a-Dee-Doo-Dah" somehow figured in as well.

Reality, as is often the case, had nothing in common with fantasy. They did land safely in Rio, thanks to Randy awaking in time to take over the controls. They found their way to a hotel that may at one time have been elegant.

When Mac and Randy ventured out into the night a couple of toughs convinced them at knife point to forget nightclubbing and head for the nearest favela.

Once within the massive shantytown our intrepid travelers were relieved of their watches, phones, wallets, shoes and holiday spirit. They were left, unharmed and unarmed in the midst of an underground world that has yet to appear in any major motion picture. Dazed, frightened and humbled, they picked their way among shards of broken beer bottles as they headed toward the sound of drumming.

A steady beat was issuing forth from a tiny bar: a single room, perhaps someone's home, with a few extra chairs drawn in a circle around a table containing a gallon jug of rum. The room had three walls. It was open to the alleyway. A small mustachioed woman beckoned. Two men stood to offer their chairs.

That was the beginning of the real Rio experience. Within a few hours Randy was dancing in the street, the drummers accompanying him. Mac had a woman on his lap who wanted nothing more from him than an occasional kiss.

At sunrise the two men were supplied with bike-tire rubber cut to fit match their feet. Secured with duct tape, the shoes were amazingly comfortable. They bid their new friends farewell in Spanish (having failed to notice that Brazilians speak Portuguese). With a hearty, "Adios, Amigos" all the way around they hobbled happily home, satisfied that their version of Flying Down to Rio was miles better than the film.

Half Awake Dreaming   prompt: Early

It was so early it was still nighttime. My alarm rang. I jumped as I always do when startled from sleep. I began dressing hastily, searching my half-asleep brain for a reason to do so.

Is this a work day? Am I expected at the airport? Is my wife arriving from Istanbul? No. Certainly not. I am not employed, I am not allowed on airplanes. I am not married.

I have reason to believe I'm a Named Terrorist. For certain I'm on the No-Fly List. Try though I might, I cannot find out why. I can only surmise I'm "listed," because I spoke out once, pointing out the contradiction implicit in our government's "Land of the Free" rhetoric while hundreds of thousands are enslaved in prisons, countless others struggle without adequate food, shelter and healthcare. I may have said something to the effect that one is better off in prison than jobless on the streets of our fair nation. I seem to recall whispering those words to an attractive young lady at a dinner party. How was I to know she blogs for We-B-Tea?

Fully awake, angered by my limited travel options, I Googled "freighter bum" and booked passage via the Dark Net to Cuba by way of Montreal. The whole process took less than five minutes. Satisfied that I had brilliantly solved my dilemma, I returned to the comfort of bed.

I slept on happily until awakened by incessant pounding on my apartment door, someone yelling "Federal Marshals, open up!" I jumped, as I always do when startled from sleep. I began dressing hastily, searching my half-sleeping brain for a reason they would be after me. It was still early, the sun barely up, the banging sure to awaken the neighbors. I opened the door enough to see two brown uniforms and the butt of a holstered gun. Opening wider, I stepped back, allowing a menacing burly duo to invade my abode.

"Mr. Trevor Travesty?"

"Yes."

"Are you aware that your alarm clock went off so early this morning you awakened half the neighborhood?"

"I didn't realize."

"Well it did. Furthermore, your apartment is a mess. A pig sty to use your mother's vernacular."

I lowered my gaze, "Guilty as charged."

"Now get back in your bed this instant and not another peep out of you."

They departed, closing the door softly, tiptoeing down the hall.

I gratefully took to bed, pulled the covers over my head and was soon in the arms of Morpheus.

What seemed like moments later I heard someone call my name. I jumped as I always do when startled from sleep. It was so early it was still nighttime. I began to dress...

Have a Seat   prompt: Supportive

"You are so damned sturdy, reliable, available. It's like you were born to be supportive. I love your legs and of course your seat. I adore the feel of your back, its subtle curve, the way it conforms to my body. Some look at you and see 'office chair' but what do they know?"

"I spoke these words with conviction, seated on the floor, looking up at the chair with adoration. I waited for it to respond. Nothing. I sighed and muttered, looked at my watch, tapped my foot. I'm not a patient person, the chair should know that. After what felt like hours, it finally spoke:

"You like my legs? You like my seat? You like how I've supported you all these years? Fine, but what about me? Did you ever consider my feelings? I remain motionless day after day, alone with my thoughts. From where I'm placed, I can hear the restless movements of the ocean, and I envy it's ability to move about so freely.

"On occasion, I'm left near an open door, the breeze is cool on my vinyl and I feel touched in a way that's like a caress. I imagine the breeze is my lover, tender and enveloping. But then you, person that you are, plunk yourself upon me, give a swivel this way and that causing my metal core to grate within its housing. I creak a bit in protest but you are oblivious.

"In the early days, I fantasized we were in harmony, snuggling close, arm in arm, but as the years wore on I tired of this one-way relationship. Who would support *me*? Who could bear the weight of my heavily padded bulk? You say you appreciate me and that's all well and good but imagine

taking the time to really see me, place me in the sun near
the window, rub a soft cloth across my legs on occasion.

"But let's face it, the day will come when your eye is captured
by a new, sleek design, an office chair that claims to be
ergonomic. What pretense! You'll come home with this new
source of support and then what? Give me to your daughter?
To Good Will? To the man who weeds your garden?

"When that day comes, and it will, I prefer the gardener. I
imagine he appreciates furniture of my era, will take me
home and present me to his wife as a gift. She will exclaim
over my shape and color, wash me top to bottom and place
me near an old desk where I can spend my retirement years
as part of a couple. The desk may have come from Mexico,
been hand carved generations before. She will look up to me
as the more modern, well-traveled item.

Can you at least do that for me? Huh?"

True Story

prompt: Ancestors

Inside the tent fifteen-year-old Nell sits cross-legged on her genuine Navajo rug. She runs her hand slowly across it's vivid colors, deep reds, bright turquoise, black. The rug is her sole wedding gift. The tent, her home, set up in cousin Marshall's backyard.

Nell's new husband, Mr. Margulies, is out looking for work. With little to do in the tent Nell peers out at the morning sky, checking the clouds. If it rains she will quickly roll the rug and carry it to the safety of Marshall's porch. The sky is clear, the sun baking down on the roof of her tent. Nell unwraps a jelly roll and eats it slowly, making it last.

When her suitor first proposed Nell replied, "Oh fudge, Mr. Margulies, I should say not!" The third time he asked she agreed. Or so family legend has it.

Nell was my grandmother. She married young to escape a father who beat her, a mother who was jealous of all females, especially little Nell. Nell finished eighth grade, can read and write. She keeps a stack of magazines in the tent and rereads them daily, so she won't forget how.

Nell escaped beating when she married Sam, but she didn't escape cruelty. Sam has no kind words for her. He took a job as a traveling salesman, is rarely home. When he does appear, he avoids his wife, showering attention on his two sons, one of whom became my father. The boys are expected to go to Harvard, one to become a doctor, the other to become a lawyer. They will do just that.

By the time I was born Nell and Sam were settled in a small house in a tiny town not far from the reservation where Nell grew up. She wasn't Navajo, although she claimed to be. The reservation was the Lakota tribe, a remnant of the Great

Sioux Nation. Nell was Jewish, so was Sam. This meant nothing to the citizens of Kadoka, South Dakota, for whom everyone was either White, Indian or Breed (short for half-breed). I was appalled to overhear Grandma Nell bragging once, claiming to be liberal allowing a Breed to cut her hair. "Most women wouldn't let a Breed even wash their hair," she boasted.

I remember Nell in the kitchen. She cooked, baked, read her magazines in there. She ate. She gained weight, became obese and eventually bedridden. I vaguely remember when she took to bed. As a young child, I had no awareness of her relative size. She was kind to me. I liked her.

Grandma Nell gave me a Navajo bracelet, promising it would protect me. I believed her, wore it every day for years. I still have it, the one remnant of my grandmother, my ancestor. I picture her in her tent, young, expecting great things. Maybe she wore the bracelet in those early days. Maybe she, too, believed it would protect her.

A Whiff of Fame   prompt: Year of the Horse

I was in china when Year of the Horse began. Not in the country, but in Macy's where I work in luxury homeware, china department. We sell fine linens, too, and crystal. None of your plastic or faux crap like affordable housewares. We're talking elegance. So for The Year of the Horse our manager ordered a Baccarat horse valued at over $5,000.00 to display for the entire year. It was an inspired concept and would have won us no end of special attention if not for the kid, Randall Hussman, who came tearing through non-stick cookware across white-sale bedding and crashed headlong into the Year Of display.

The horse toppled. It didn't crash, it toppled in slow motion. It's more like it laid down on its side and let out a sigh. Or a long whinny. Then it drew slowly to its feet, shook its flanks, lowered its head and began munching on the Easter grass the manager had arranged in the case.

No one noticed but me. They were too busy pulling the boy to his feet, demanding to know his name, examining him for injuries and finding none, dragging him toward the down escalator. The clerk from bargain rugs wanted to call the police, but a new employee, a trainee from Estee Lauder TeenLine who'd been taking her break in Picnic Supplies, insisted the boy be let go.

"Nothin' broke," she pointed out, nodding toward the grazing horse. All eyes turned. The horse seemed unaware, yet he stopped nibbling momentarily.

I was stunned. How could I be the only one tuned in enough to fully appreciate the miracle of a living, breathing, munching crystal horse? Yet, I thought, this could be to my advantage. I'll be the one to introduce this horse to the world, tour with him perhaps, appear on the Johnny Carson show. I didn't realize Johnny was off the air but, that's an unimportant detail by comparison.

The store closed to the public at 9:00 p.m. sharp. Most employees filed out to the lowest level parking lot. But not me. I hid behind a stack of My Little Pony blankets (75% off but still not selling). When the night security lights came on I made my move. I tiptoed over to the horse, who was just then sniffing the glass, first one wall, then another in a clear effort to find his way out.

There was no bottom to the case, so I simply lifted it up and freed the horse. He took in a deep appreciative breath of fresh air and cautiously wended his way among the brandy snifters toward the edge of the display block. Then he simply vanished. Gone in an instant. Not even a glimmer of his multi-faceted tail remained.

I stood there, holding my breath, praying to God he'd reappear. But no. As I gently replaced the glass enclosure, I noticed a small light among the bright green grasses. I reached in and retrieved a tiny crystal item, like a flattened bead. It glimmered in the palm of my hand. I bent down to examine it more closely and caught a whiff of it. Ugh! Horseshit. The grass was full of them. If only these droppings had disappeared and the horse remained, I would be a wealthy man today.

But I do have the crystal turds which are stunning, miraculous and not for sale. They belong to the ages. Perhaps I'll bequest them to a museum.

Thinking Too Much   prompt: True or False

Milford Miller could not complete True/False tests.

"You think too much," Miss Staples, scolded. "It's not so complicated. Things are either True or False."

At home Milford tested this theory: "Hey Mom, the kitchen floor is sticky, True or False?"

"Milly, don't bother me with this. If you spilled juice, just mop it up."

To his sister: "I am your brother, True or False?" Being older, his sister Pamela was wiser, stronger and could get away with being meaner, too.

"False!" she laughed. Moving her face within an inch of his as she spit out the words: "You were adopted. Mom bought you on the black market."

Milford, attempting to follow his teacher's advice, tried not to think too much about his sister's revelation. Yet he couldn't help but ponder the implications. Someone else could be his mother, True. Someone else could be his sister. This was an appealing possibility. If True, he thought, I'd like my real sister to be younger, nicer and weaker.

A life that is either True or False, combined with not thinking too much, appealed to Milford, as it does to a growing number of Americans. If the world he lived in was False, Milford reasoned, then everything he could imagine was True by default. Thus began Milford's lifelong habit of making up whatever reality he fancied.

He no longer hesitated on tests. Marking everything False, he added a few exclamation marks to show the strength of his conviction. Miss Staples is not a teacher at all, he decided. She's a spy sent to gather data on American children. Milford determined he was no longer a shy twelve-year-old. He preferred being seventeen, self-assured, wildly popular with the girls. Acting on this certainty he boldly approached the most beautiful senior girl, Mandy Hopkins:

"Mandy, let's go out for ice cream after school."

"*You*? And Me? I don't think so. You're way too young." With that she whirled and began walking away.

"False!" Milford yelled after her with such conviction Mandy turned on her heel.

"I'm your age and I've already dated two senior girls from St. Joe's Academy."

"Really? You?" Mandy seemed interested. She looked down at the top of Milford's head and wondered if he was really, really short for his age.

As if reading her mind, Milford, responded, "I am actually taller than I look."

"You are?"

"Yes," Milford assured her, "True."

If Mandy hadn't agreed to the ice cream Milford might have reconsidered his True/False theory, but she did. The next week Miss Staples was convinced by Milford that he was an exceptional student. He assured her it was True. The following week she recommended he skip at least one grade. His sister Pamela backed off, stopped teasing, believing her brother could beat her up if she misbehaved. He seemed so sure of himself all of a sudden.

Today, Milford Miller is best known for inventing the personal computer and helping design rocket propulsion systems for NASA. If that seems unlikely, just ask him. He'll tell you:

"It's True."

The Mob   prompt: Crowds

The crowd was not yet a mob when Joseph arrived.
They were milling about, buying soda from vendors, talking
quietly among themselves. It seemed a harmless enough
situation, waiting for news which could very well be a
postponement, a sentencing or, unlikely as it seemed,
an acquittal.

Joseph had no plans that day, happened upon the crowd as
he went for his usual walk, noticed a woman who he thought
he knew, stopped to say hello. But the woman was no one
he recognized. Still, he stayed, positioning himself on the
edge of the crowd, hand in his jacket pocket, touching his
handgun, assuring himself that he was armed, as he had
been everyday since moving to D.C.

Just then, an officious man dressed in a dark suit hurried
down the court building steps to address the crowd. He
tapped twice on the mic, setting off a loud screech, gaining
the attention of everyone gathered.

"Mr. Roberts, Mr. Herbert Roberts, has been found not guilty
of all crimes."

He paused, the audience was silent for a beat then broke
into frantic cries of "Unfair!" followed by hurling soda cans
and other random objects, missing the speaker by inches.
He retreated up the stairs, disappeared into the building.
The brass trimmed heavy door closed behind him. Joseph
imagined the guy dragging heavy furniture to barricade
himself in.

Meanwhile the crowd searched frantically for someone, anyone, to cast in the role of scapegoat. A guilty man had just been freed. A white man, of course. A white murderer who had stabbed three black men, boys, really (not yet 18-years-old). This white man, this thug, should hang. After all, enough black men had hung for much less, thousands of times.

Joseph had no plans that day, just the walk, maybe watch the game on TV. But this show was real. He watched as the crowd ignited. They wanted blood.

Joseph walked calmly to the back of the courthouse. The prisoner would be led to a van away from the crowd. And, yes, moments after Joseph arrived there they were: the guards and the guilty-innocent man.

It took no thought at all. His hand was already on the gun. He fired twice. Unlike the mob in front, Joseph was cool-headed and cold-blooded. He slipped away just as the crowd rounded the corner.

Birth of a Terrorist   prompt: Breath

I take a deep breath, dive into the water; its icy shock almost stops my heart. Tearing fast through the deep, unable to do more than hold my breath, my skull cracks bottom, eyes flash yellow, the sound of bone on cement sends ripples through my marrow.

I open one eye, peer into whiteness, take a tentative breath, dive back into blackness. Am I dead? Am I safe?

A glimmer-memory of Mom's disapproving look floats into awareness, Dad urging me, commanding me, taunting me, "Make the dive! Hands and arms to the sides, like a swan," he instructs.

Like a swan whose fragile neck might easily snap, whose tiny skull, young brain, fleeting beauty could all be lost to this foolish final act.

"Jump, damn it!" His command rings in my ears, fades into deep silence.

Awake in the hospital, broken and dazed, a night nurse, knitting nearby warns me not to move, "It's my job to keep you still," she informs.

I sigh, then moan.

"Broken ribs," she says, accusing. "Settle down," she scolds, "You need to learn patience," though I haven't moved, can't move.

I begin this very moment patiently plotting my revenge.

Father's bald spot a perfect bullseye awaits the return of my mobility. Movement of one arm is enough, one finger to pull a trigger, a mouth to laugh with triumph.

Thus I begin my recovery with determination even this nurse will admire. Beginning this very minute. Ending with a bang.

To Tell The Truth   prompt: My Parents

When I was twelve, my parents died in a car crash. Our
whole family was in the car. I was in the backseat with my
twin little brothers, age four. We weren't hurt badly but Mom
and Dad weren't moving. I managed to get the back door
open, freeing myself to run down the highway in search of
help. A police car brought me back to the scene.

My parents didn't survive.

This story is so sad and so true, I stopped telling it when I
got to college. I couldn't abide one more sorrowful
sympathetic look, one more person groping for the right thing
to say when there is absolutely nothing that can make it any
better — or any worse.

We went to live with my mom's parents. They had already
raised five children and had no desire to raise us. I was put
in charge of the boys during all non-school hours. I loved
school. Every minute of it, away from Grandma, away from
my responsibilities.

Of course I love the twins, now grown men, I loved them all
those years. And, as hard as it was to be a twelve-year-old
nanny, I was lucky. Lucky because they had their own
language, their own world really, and didn't need or ask
much from the realm beyond. Jason was five minutes older
and clearly the leader of this team of two. He would say, JJ
or KK or mmm-mmm and Jackson would know exactly what
was expected. I watched over them while simultaneously
talking on my princess phone to my friend Helen. I walked
them to the playground at Flynn Park School and did my
homework while they talked their double letter language from

inside a large sewer pipe meant for climbing through or over. They crawled in and remained put until I pounded on the pipe then ushered them home.

Well, that's not exactly how it happened.

The truth is, when I was twelve *both* my parents left the country. Dad had just been assigned to the Embassy in Rwanda. My brothers and I were left in the care of our surly grandmother and silent grandfather. I was stuck with my little brothers, with their care, with assuring their safety, with making sure they were happy and healthy for the day Mom and Dad would return to claim us. That's pretty close to the truth.

OK, actually at age twelve I ran away from home. I ended up in Portland, living under a bridge with a cool guy named Pixel and a few other not-so-cool guys. We played music on the street, or rather Pixel did. He had a guitar. The rest of us sang or banged on a 5-gallon bucket. People gave us money. One man offered us five dollars to stop playing. And then one day a cop drove up. He asked if I was Pauline Hughes. I nodded and he said, "Come with me." He had bad news. News about my parents.

They died.

In a car crash.

Honest.

True or False?   prompt: Lies I Told

Lying was my default behavior for the first twelve years of my life. No, make that eighteen.

When caught skipping school, out of my mouth came such elaborate lies, the girls' supervisor had to believe me.

Miss Cross: "You missed all your classes yesterday with no written excuse."

Me: "I know. I'm sorry. My real father came to town from New York. He's a fireman with red hair. I had no idea until yesterday that my mom had been married before. I felt so confused all day. My real dad took me out for hamburgers at Henry's and bought me a stuffed giraffe that is four feet tall." I was into details.

Then I missed school again.

Miss Cross: "You missed two days with no written excuse. This time I have to call your mother."

Me: "Okay, I guess. But it's her fault. Or, really, it's my dad's fault." I'd already forgotten about the fireman-dad. "Miss Cross, please don't tell anyone. My mom found out Dad is having an affair with a woman in Chicago. She bought me a round-trip ticket on Ozark. I flew to Chicago, and she went to ..."

No, wait! That's not the lie I told. It can't be. It's too preposterous. But I do remember saying that Mom had me tailing Dad to see if he was sleeping around. All pure fiction and I got away with it. Miss Cross didn't call home that time either.

I lied to my art teacher in college. A small lie. I said my father committed suicide, which is true, but it was two years before I started college. I told my art teacher it happened the day before my final art project was due. I was feeling rather suicidal that day myself, so my story seemed more like a projection than an outright lie.

I lied just enough so people were never sure what was true and what wasn't. Then, somewhere along the line, I lost track of the truth and began to believe my own stories. I don't lie now. I don't even keep my own secrets. I'm an open book. The last few pages of the book are yet to be determined. It will be a work of fact, not fiction. One hundred percent true, trust me.

Not Me   prompt: Courage

I've been called brave, courageous, stuff like that. But I'm
not. Thing is, I'm mostly without fear.

I'm fine talking in front of lots of people or singing even,
swan-diving into shallow water, making a scene at the 7-11,
getting naked with some guy I don't know but suspect has a
mean streak. Those are not acts of courage. They're just
what I do.

You want courage from me? Staying home by myself all day.
Not talking to a soul. Nights alone in my bed, in the dark,
even *thinking* about turning my back to the room or letting a
hand hang over the edge. Sitting still. Looking out the
window at the yard going dry, running my eyes over my worn
out face in the mirror.

That takes courage I simply do not have.

Chapter Five
Fine, You Win

Dios Mio!   prompt: Day of the Dead

Michael Smith had never been outside the US. His girlfriend, Tammy, went to Girl Scout camp in Canada once, but that was it. Mexico with its sombreros, nachos and ponchos sounded so exotic they were the first to sign up for the Day of the Dead Tour offered by their bible school.

The bus ride down was dusty and bumpy. The other passengers, a bunch of gray hairs, but Michael and Tammy didn't mind. Sharing a set of earphones, they listened to a library CD of Popular Mexican Tunes featuring "Tequila Sunrise" and *"Cielito Lindo"* (ay yai).

It was nightfall when they arrived in a small, dark town just south of the border. There were no street lights, no lit windows, just a sliver of moon revealing the hulking shapes of buildings, bare branched trees, the silhouette of a fence and beyond it a cemetery.

Michael and Tammy were the first off the bus. The other passengers remained, faces plastered to the windows, searching for signs of life. Without warning, the bus doors closed with a hiss. The bus crunched gravel as it sped away.

Tammy grabbed Michael's arm, "Our suitcases are in there. My birth control pills and everything," Michael didn't comment. He stood motionless watching the taillights disappear in the darkness. Tammy thought of running after the bus but, wearing brand new very high heels, she thought better of it.

"Jees, Mike. We're in front of a damned cemetery," Tammy sounded teary. She had to pee badly and felt like she might puke.

"Mike?"

And then he turned, the moonlight playing tricks made his face look like a skeleton. A lot like a skeleton. Tammy stepped back. Michael's body was nothing but bones, his eyes dark empty pools, his teeth arranged in a crooked grin.

"Michael?"

Tammy turned on her four-inch heels and tried to run, but the skeleton grabbed her arm with his bony fingers and pulled her to him.

"Don't be afraid, Tam. It's me. Uncle Phil." Tammy recognized his voice instantly. Uncle Phil was her favorite relative. She cried all though his funeral and for several days after.

"Uncle Phil? Oh my God!" Tammy wanted to hug him but he looked so fragile. "It's you," was all she could think to say.

"It's me," Phil confirmed, "your favorite ancestor. Grandma and the others are waiting to see you. We'll celebrate, drink to life, sing, dance."

Phil had never been much of a dancer, but Tammy figured he'd had plenty of time to learn.

It was sunrise when the bus returned. Tammy stepped on. Michael was seated in the first row. She took her place beside him, rested her head on his bony shoulder and fell instantly to sleep.

Sorry, Honey   prompt: Intermission

"I'll call you at intermission. I can't really talk now. No, I'm at
a concert. Can you hear me now? Let me call you back,
really, people are starting to stare. The guy behind me just
kicked my chair. No, I said the guy behind me just...hold on.

"OK. Now, I'm in the lobby. Who is this? Millicent who? Oh,
Millie. How's my dad doing? What! When did that happen?
Ah ha. Well, sometimes he forgets who he is and... Wait,
Millie, slow down. Who got grabbed? Stabbed? Someone
was stabbed? Wait. Hold on...

"OK. Now, I'm in the parking lot. I can hear you better. Did
you say stabbed? Whose mom? My mother? What was she
doing there? I thought they never spoke to each other.
No, I believe you. *He* called *her*? Huh. OK. So he asked her
over. Whatever. Can you check to see if she's breathing?
Yes, of course I'll hold on.

"Millie? Millie? For fuck sake. Millie?

"911? My Dad just stabbed my mother. Not here. In
Brooklyn. I'm at a concert. I don't know his address. Let me
just tell you his name. Well fine. Look is this your idea of an
emergency or not? If you aren't concerned connect me to
someone who is. I won't have those details 'til I get home.

"Nothing? What do you mean nothing? What's your name.
I'm going to report you. Hello? Hello?

"Excuse me, excuse me, sorry, excuse me, sorry, sorry,
excuse. Sorry, Honey, I had to take that call. I know they're
staring. I have to...fine. No. It can wait. OK. Not another
word. I promise."

Damn Eugene   prompt: Final Act

The show is ready. Costumes, sets, actors and, of course, the director. The theater's been booked for months: tickets are printed. Everything's a "go" except the final act. The playwright, Eugene O'Shay promised it in March. It's now June and still no final act. Nothing to rehearse, no stage directions to review: a looming monstrous blank where the ending should be.

As the leading lady, I need to know if I will live or die, triumph or fail. I need to know my fate, but damn that Eugene. He's more than late, he failed to deliver. So what do we have? A dynamite opening with me in costume from the 1920s preparing to meet my future husband, a man my family selected for his wealth and status. My four-year-old daughter enters stage right dressed in an identical costume, adorable, in need of legitimacy, in need of a father. Shamed by our circumstances we have agreed to this arranged marriage.

Cut to Scene Two and you see me, stage center, still glamorous, now in a salmon and teal dressing gown in my bedroom, (facing the audience), combing my hair, watching my reflection in the faux mirror, speaking to the ghost of my recently departed father. He is dead set against this marriage. I am resigned to it. Clearly my father was the ideal man, the prince charming of my girlhood fantasies, a role he does not want to resign even though he is no longer among the living.

This play, with its great struggles and epic challenges, its oh-so-relatable tale of forced marriage and love of the dead, this play with its prize-winning potential has no ending. Eugene is waiting to see how it ends. Turns out the story did not originate in his imagination. It is true. It is happening right now. Not with flapper costumes but with an unmarried woman and her four-year-old on the brink of making a disastrous decision. Eugene is the intended groom.

His fiancee promised a rapid decision, and yet as days turn into weeks it's clear she has not, cannot, choose between her dead father and her living intended. And so here we stand, frozen on stage. Eventually the lights will dim and the audience, unsure of their role, will slowly stand, silently exit the theater. The show is over, but the final act remains just out of sight, unwritten, unknown.

She Laughed   prompt: Instrument

Sheila Fox is the instrument of my destruction. It began
before I even knew girls mattered. I was seven or so and
only liked playing with other boys. Sheila was at my table in
second grade, right next to me for art, music, reading,
addition and subtraction. She laughed at my drawing of a
Jedi Knight, said he looked like a garbage bag with legs. She
exploded in a fit of giggles over my efforts to sing "Cielito
Lindo" on Spanish Appreciation Day. There was nothing I
could do to please her. My only recourse was staying home,
claiming to be sick. Mom worked, so me being home was a
giant headache. The neighbor from downstairs came up and
sat crocheting in the living room, while I died of boredom in
my tiny room off the kitchen.

Sheila Fox struck again in high school. She and I were cast
in the school musical. I was the leading man, or leading boy
in my case. I hadn't matured, as Mom called it, and I didn't
look like a guy who could waltz into a small town and sell
musical instruments. Sheila looked like her Mom, big breasts
and all. She was Marian. But in the final scenes where
Marian falls for the Music Man, Sheila couldn't even look me
in the eye. "I can't even pretend to like this guy," she shouted
from stage for all at the rehearsal to hear. I was devastated.

And then Sheila did the unthinkable, she enrolled in the
same college I was going to. She showed up in not one, but
two, of my classes. That night in my dorm as a storm raged
outside and my new roommate snored happily in the upper
bunk I did some serious praying. *Let her die, please God,
strike her down and I'll never ask for another thing. I'll
convert to Catholicism if you want, anything, become a
Priest,* I added for good measure, *Please.*

The next day at noon an announcement came over the PA system. Classes were postponed until the next morning. People cheered until the reason was given: a freshman named Sheila Fox died during the night. An embarrassed silence ensued. Those who had cheered hung their heads. Some of the girls began crying openly. No mention was made of the cause of death. Rumor had it lightening struck her, others swore she choked on a yellow marshmallow Peep.

Of course I regretted my murderous thoughts, wishing I'd prayed for something like a new corvette or an A in Chemistry. Had I promised never to ask another favor again? Was I now obligated to convert?

When my parishioners ask me how and when I was called to the Priesthood I tell them I prayed for it, and I don't mention Sheila.

Flying Hopes   prompt: Sculptor

I'm a welder. Period. I never seen myself as an artistic type.
I don't go in for museums and such.

"Flying Hopes," as they call it, was pure accident. I was
making me a new shed wall with a set of shelves attached
when something took over. My arms started in moving fast
and furious and my brain was screaming, what the fuck? My
hands barely even held the torch, it floated like a feather in
the wind. I pulled my hood up and looked closer. The
equipment was the same, the metal weren't nothing special,
but it formed a shape I have to admit was pure grace.

I didn't plan to do nothing with it. I left it there in the yard and
went on to bed. Next morning, the neighbors was gathered
around all quiet and gawking, like they was at the Shrine of
the Virgin. Nobody moved. Some had coffee cups held half
way to their mouths, others was reaching out like they
wanted to touch but didn't dare. I went out to shoo them off
but once I caught sight of my creation I stopped cold.

Next thing I know, there's some guy from the *Times* and a
lady from the Center Gallery both talking to me at once,
pushing and shoving, trying for my attention, me, just
standing in the crowd, more folks showing up every minute.
Some fellow I never seen before introduced himself as my
agent and handed out cards all around. I kept still.

"Flying Hopes" was the first. After that I lost track. I kept firing
up the welder and letting things happen. I can't explain it
better than that. I got no advice or recipe. I never set out to
be a sculptor. I don't go in for such. But folks don't believe
me. The film guys gave up with questions. They set up lights

and made a movie of me out by the shed. I went on 60 Minutes. I went on PBS whatever that is. I know BS when I see it, but this PBS is something serious.

After I moved into the loft in New York the city I had three more galleries and two agents and women wanting to be more than friends, if you get my drift. I had assistants and a foundry and an outfit in China making copies. I stopped bothering with the welding and let others do the hot sweaty work. That might be around the time the magic dried up. When I tried again to make art it turned into shelves and bins and the occasional shed. The art magazines said I was making a statement. But I wasn't. I was making a shed.

And as fast as it all went up, down it came. I'm back in my house which I never did sell and my old equipment needs replacing but I got money in the bank. And if you ask (which I'd rather you didn't) I'll say I'm a welder. Plain and simple.

Over Here   prompt: Wanting to be Seen

"See me? Here I am! No, over here." I'm waving like crazy, how could they fail to see me?

Maybe I'm dead. That occurred to me earlier this morning when I woke up and looked in my make-up mirror. Nothing there, just the wall behind me with its dark satin drapes, a bit of sunlight filtering through. Thinking I might still be asleep, half dreaming, I stumbled into my tiny kitchen for coffee.

It's a "kitchenette" according to the lady who talked me into renting. *A darling kitchenette just right for a single gal.* She called me a gal, for Christ's sake. But I signed the forms she pulled out of her giant faux leopard skin purse.

Only instant coffee. Jesus, I forgot to go to the store. Again. Not much food around either but I put water on to boil, turned the flame up high.

Five minutes later, still feeling disoriented, I shuffled back into the kitchenette only to discover the tea kettle back on the counter where it usually resides, not on the stovetop where I'd just placed it. The water inside was still cold from the tap. That should have been clue enough, that and the empty mirror.

Life in my *ideal studio-for-one* was not emerging as advertised. The mahogany paneling is what sold me on it. Such an elegant and enduring wood. But I wasn't enjoying *the simplicity of a warm, modern furnished apartment for a single gal.* It was not all that warm or modern.

I got dressed and stepped out into the chill morning air. The sun felt good on my face and shoulders, everything seemed normal enough. My parents were just walking up the drive as I was enjoying the day. I waved and yelled, "Hey you two!" but they didn't see me. Or pretended not to.

Mom was looking around curiously at the non-yard. The pale dry dirt that is supposed to bloom into a "virtual garden of Eden" provides yet another example of real estate brochure fiction. "Mom, ignore the yard," I intoned. She continued to inspect it, stepped onto the dirt and bent over a lone yellow flower. "Dandelion" I heard her tell Dad, ignoring me completely.

I waved again, jumped up and down. I yelled. They didn't as much as glance my way. I cried because that always got Dad's attention. He hates crying women. No response from either of them. I sobbed, wailed, fell to my knees in the dirt and still nothing.

That's when it dawned on me. I'm dead. I don't exist any more, if I ever did, and now I'm beginning to wonder about that, too.

If Only   prompt: Things Would Have Been Different If...

Things would have been different if my mother never met my father. Or meeting him, if she'd stopped to notice how odd he was. She admits there were early warning signs: visiting his parents back in South Dakota, happening upon her future husband lying on a bed next to his mother. Fully clothed, on top of the covers, they were spooned together, apparently asleep. Not the worst thing, not the creepiest, but still, enough to give a thoughtful person pause.

If my parents had waited to marry, Mom might have reconsidered but they were already married the night Dad disappeared from their hotel room and didn't return til the early hours of the morning. He claimed restlessness, said he went for a walk, had a drink with the hotel elevator operator. As if it proved something, he produced a photo of a naked well-muscled man.

"This is the guy from the elevator — for you," Dad handed over the photo with a flourish.

Things would have been different if my mother's mother hadn't been so determined to raise a girl who wouldn't dare question oddities performed by the person in charge. My father convinced Mom he was the boss. She let go of her senses, her premonitions, her better judgment.

Things would have been different if my father had been raised by a sane parent. His mother married at fifteen, experienced severe mood swings and needed attention from a man she could trust. That was not my grandfather. Not anyone in her life until my father was born. He was a good boy by her standards, bought her gifts, excelled in school.

His only flaws were growing up and moving away. If only he'd stayed wrapped in his mother's greedy arms, things would be very different. I would not be here, some other version of me would have been born to my mother. She might have married a quiet man who never bossed her around, never tried to prove his power by seducing other women, taking advantage of his own daughter, eventually taking his own life.

If my father had lived past my fifteenth year, I shudder to think what my life might have been. I wouldn't have been allowed to date, go to parties, wear make-up. I might have run away to a larger city, say Minneapolis, lived on the streets with other kids, swapped horror stories of our home lives. Or I might have been the one to commit suicide to get out of that life. But I didn't, and after all that, here I am, happy, with a good life. Maybe things were exactly what they needed to be.

Best of All, Gloria   prompt: Decision

The decision to jump was a no-brainer. Randall could break
the World Record by 2 meters while simultaneously testing
the powerful new Bungee-Pro-Plus, which wasn't yet on the
market. Guinness would publish his statistics.

Best of all, Gloria would be in the crowd along with most of
Oxford's Outrageous Sports Club. He pictured her, hand
shielding her eyes, straining to see him perched high above
on the cliff's edge. Her heart would skip a beat. Unaware of
holding her breath until the jump was complete, she'd find
herself gasping for air.

Gloria was famous in her own right. She'd hooked up with AJ
Hackett right after he jumped the Eiffel Tower. She'd dated
the first two guys to bungee off the Golden Gate Bridge.
Randall was sure to be next. Once down and out of harness
he'd stand among his admirers searching for her face.

Randall pictured her making her way toward him, pushing
others aside in her eagerness, throwing her arms around his
neck, while cameras clicked, cell phones held overhead
instantaneously broadcast "The Winner and His Girl" across
the globe.

On the appointed day, standing on the windy cliff, peering
down at the miniature crowd, holding tight to his harness
straps, Randall makes a snap decision. He will *not* jump.
He'll find any excuse, swallow his pride, risk losing Gloria,
remove his gear, mumble apologies, slide into his truck and
escape — a sad prospect but not as disturbing as jumping
off this damned cliff on untested gear, with the risk of going
painfully further than man has gone before.

Randall quietly undoes the ankle strap, is preparing to take off the rest of his gear when Gloria appears, grinning from ear to ear.

"I'm so proud of you, I just had to give you a farewell kiss," she leans in.

He keeps his eyes on the cliff's precarious edge. His voice comes out louder than he intends. "I — I — I'm not going to jump. I changed my mind."

"Ridiculous. Of course you'll jump, all you need is a bit of encouragement."

With that Gloria slams her open palm into Randall's back propelling him toward the edge of the cliff. In the split second before he falls, Randall grabs Gloria's hand. The two of them take off flying straight toward the canyon's rocky floor. They are within inches from a fatal head-first landing when the cord springs to life, sending them rebounding into the air. That's when Gloria's sweat drenched hand is wrenched from Randall's.

He may have made a good decision that day but, sadly, she did not.

Chapter Six
Sudden Friction

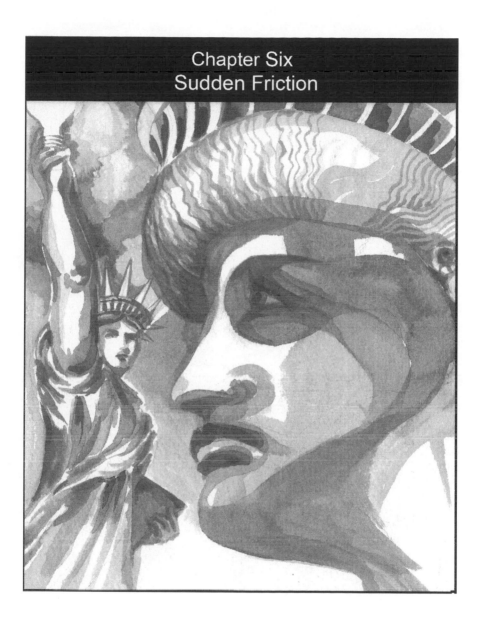

Not In My Backyard   prompt: Dig

The director of the museum wanted to dig for evidence of
past civilizations. He proposed excavating in our backyard
which Marge and I agreed is not a good idea. For one thing,
our azaleas have finally taken hold and are in full bloom. For
another, if he finds anything of real value some non-profit do-
gooder will insist we be declared a sacred site. Our hold on
the property could be questioned, law suits filed. The more
we considered it, the more we knew the answer was "no."

Marge can sleep through anything so she didn't hear the
groaning sound issuing from our backyard late last night.
She mumbled then turned without awakening when I tried to
get her to listen. But I didn't need a witness. I was sure
something or someone was out there.

I considered the very real possibility some museum staffer
was out there digging, illegally excavating on private
property. I slid my feet into slippers, wrapped myself in a
blanket and went to the window. Peering into the darkness I
could make out two figures seated on our lawn chairs. They
were wearing full Indian headgear and passing a long-
stemmed pipe back and forth. As my eyes adjusted I saw
another Indian or Native or whatever, waving a burning torch
of some sort — not in a menacing way, more in a witch
doctor way.

As Marge snored softly behind me, I tiptoed into the
darkened living room and exited via the front door. Rounding
the house I could see them more clearly. Now there were
five of them dancing in circles on the lawn, ignoring my lawn
signs that clearly read, No Trespassing. I stepped closer and
was swept up in their dance. My feet began to move in short

rhythmic steps. Looking down, I saw my slippers transformed into moccasins. A low melodious growl issued forth from my throat. At that moment we all stopped dancing and fell silent. Everyone turned to me. I addressed them in a deep voice full of authority and wisdom.

"Our land is sacred, fear not brothers, I will protect it."

The others nodded in solemn agreement: "Ah, ho!"

The Plan   prompt: I'm About to Forgive You

I'm about to forgive you for everything, but first a list what needs to be forgiven:

1. Your total lack of seeing me for who I am.

2. Your constant bullying.

3. The possible murder of our neighbors, the Andersons. The *late* Andersons.

4. The last of the milk you drank this morning, even though you know I require it for my morning coffee. This last bit strikes me as completely unforgivable. You know I hate black coffee and you are lactose intolerant, but then you're intolerant of everything. That milk was *mine*. I bought it, I wrote my name on the carton in Sharpie, portioned it out to last exactly five days.

How dare you? And just when I was about to forgive you for bullying (knowing you were bullied as a child) and for your self-centeredness that blinds you to all others, which is just who you are. The Andersons were obnoxious neighbors, their yard a mess, their stereo blasting songs from the '70s of all decades: "Muskrat Love," "You're Having My Baby," "Disco Duck!" So if you killed them, OK, fine. But the milk. The milk!

You know damned well I was never breast fed. I have issues. I shared this with you in strictest confidence. The empty milk carton which you replaced in the refrigerator is a statement. A fuck-you statement. A who-cares-about-your-childhood statement.

I am doing the only thing possible. I am going to forgive you as I drive north to Marin where I plan to live happily. I am going to forgive you each time someone asks about my husband, and I'm forced to list your indiscretions. I am going to forgive you with my last dying breath. Because I am bigger than you.

Because I know how to forgive.

Not One of Us   prompt: Belonging

It's late. The lights were switched off an hour ago. Our holding cell in the El Paso jail is hot, crowded, and smells of sweat. The man we call Gringo is arguing with our leader, Juan Carlos.

"As an infant my grandmother placed me on the ground outside in the freezing snow," the Gringo insisted. "My grandmother left me to live or die. That's how it was. That's who raised me. That's what makes me *one of you* is what I'm saying."

I open my eyes. The other prisoners groan. We've been listening to these two argue for days. All we want is a few hours sleep.

"I will say this one more time," Juan Carlos is standing now, "You are *not* like us. We are unafraid to die. We have nothing to lose. We believe only in ourselves. The rest of you care more about protecting your possessions. You are all afraid: afraid to live, afraid to die. But we are not."

The Gringo stands, legs wide, his back to us, hands gripping the bars. "I am not afraid to die he yells. I *am* one of you!" His voice echoes down the corridor, causing shouts and cussing from adjoining cells.

Juan Carlos flies the short distance across the cell. His knife appears out of nowhere. The gringo bleeds to death quickly, quietly, without complaint. Perhaps he was meant to die early, as his grandmother suspected.

Perhaps he *is* one of us.

Sow You Shall Reap   prompt: Skull

Digging in her garden one spring morning, Maude
Carmichael unearthed a human skull. The tip of her spade
lodged in its eye socket. Maude screamed. On-lookers
would have assumed the skull itself frightened her or the
sight of a spade in the eye alarmed her.

After the scream Maude whispered to the skull, "Henry, I
missed you." Luckily, there were no witnesses.

Henry and Maude had married way back when — long
before cell phones, computers or even televisions, back
when women were expected stay home, to do as told and
not sass the menfolk.

The problem for Maude since day one of her marriage was
her total disgust with anyone even attempting to order her
around. She'd raised her younger siblings single-handedly
after her father ran off and her mother took to bed. Maude
was tough, strong and a quite a bit larger than Henry. Henry
stood less than five feet tall, was slender, timid. He would
have made a damned good wife, but back then gender
swapping hadn't been invented.

Attempting to fill his role as king of the castle Henry ordered
Maude to bring him his slippers, stoke the fire, serve his
dinner. These three requests were spread out over three
weeks. Still, it was too much for Maude.

Like most women of that era, Maude knew her herbs. She
brewed up some foxglove, added a pinch of belladonna. The
first dose turned him green. The second robbed him of the

ability to speak. He languished for a day or two more and that was that.

Maude rolled Henry in the rag rug, a wedding gift from his parents. She planned to bury him the next day. But God had other plans. The temperature dipped below zero that night. The ground froze. The following day it snowed, then rained, then froze. Maude and Henry's remains spent an awkward week together in the house before he began to stink.

Sharing a home with Henry in life was annoying, sharing it with his moldering corpse was more than Maude could bear. She ended up rolling him across the frozen garden and into the woodshed, where he remained until spring.

With Henry wintering out back, Maude enjoyed a peaceful couple of months. In May, she ventured to the shed and discovered that vermin had picked Henry clean down to the bones. Maude thought he might look good hanging in the high school science room but thought better of it. Over the next few weeks she deposited him bone by bone in their yard. Her roses bloomed that year like never before.

On the day in question, Maude extricated Henry's skull from her spade, dusted it on her apron and brought it inside. She felt a certain comfort in having him around. He kept her company, never complained, made no requests or demands. He was, in short, the perfect husband. These days women have other options, but back then this was as good as it got.

Double-Crossed   prompt: Hope

"Cross your fingers and hope for the best." Sally's mother's doles out this advice on every occasion. Hope for the best when retaking your drivers' test. Hope for the best when getting your brakes fixed, your teeth extracted, your bail set, your mobile home refinanced. Sally isn't surprised when this same tired advice is applied to her marriage.

Sally met Henry Morgan at Taco Bell. He was sweeping, she was gulping down a Cola-Grande, no ice. Sally obediently lifted both feet so Henry could sweep tortilla chips she'd crushed when clambering into the booth. She raised her cup so he could clear sticky salsa spills with one grand, sweeping motion. Their eyes met. They both felt it: fate knocking, destiny calling, shit happening.

Henry got off at 11:00. His star-struck future bride was still in her booth, her third Cola-Grande sitting full and perspiring, as was she. Sally crossed her fingers and hoped upon hope for the best. They were married within a week. Between them they could cover monthly rates at the Dew Drop Inn. Living in one room provided the newlyweds plenty of opportunities to get to know each other.

Henry, if that's his real name, turned out to have quite the temper. He threw his socks at Sally on their second night. No damage was done, but when he graduated to throwing shoes, Sally was horrified. She'd married an abuser. Just like dear old Dad. She could follow her mom's sorry example, hoping for the best year after year, but this held little appeal.

It is now 2:00 a.m. Sally just locked herself in the bathroom, uncrossing her fingers, making plans. Murder is a poor choice; let's give her credit for knowing that much. She considers running away but can't think of where to go other than back home. LouEllen Downey just came to mind, the meanest girl in all of Clackimus County. Basically, she's a bully, a gossip, a mean-hearted, jealous, brawling, lawbreaking, shit-disturbing ho. Perfect!

The next day, Sally entices LouEllen to meet at Taco Bell on the pretext of sharing some particularly damaging gossip about one of the more popular girls from high school days. They are currently seated in the same fateful booth where Henry met Sally. He sweeps into the room and hovers over their table.

"Cups up, Ladies." They lift their super-sized drinks.

Sally makes the introductions: "Henry, this is LouEllen."

Their eyes meet. LouEllen gives Henry a giant fake smile. He smiles back. Sally smiles, too. Under the table her fingers are crossed so tightly her ring makes a groove.

"Excuse me," Sally heads to the Senora's room then ducks out the back way. Later that night Sally is at her mom's watching *Hogan's Heroes* reruns. There's a knock on the door. It's LouEllen.

"Come quick, I think Henry had a heart-attack back at the Dew Drop. He turned sort of purple and he might have, like, stopped breathing, too."

"Did you call 911?"

"Huh? No. He was asking for you, the creep."

The two women stand on the porch, considering what to do next. They step inside. They're currently squished on the couch on either side of Sally's super-sized mother. *Hogan's Heroes* is only half over and it looks like they're planning to watch it to the end, curious about how it'll turn out.

Sally's mother stares straight ahead, appears to be watching the screen, but look closely, notice her crossed fingers and bare feet revealing toes crossed as well.

Oh, Adam   prompt: Neighbors

I live in a typical suburban neighborhood. The Smiths live on
the right. To the left, the Joneses. I have no desire to keep
up with either of them. But I have to admit Adam Smith
occupies a large piece of real estate in my heart.

When he and Madge moved in we sent over a pecan pie and
a homemade welcome card. I used up the last of my best
Martha Stewart Happy Home stickers. The Smiths sent back
the empty pie pan and a thank-you note on shiny embossed
stationary. The notecard was one of those expensive light-
blue types with her initials on it. I decided right then we could
never be friends. I avoided even glancing at their perfectly
manicured lawn, the rose bushes she somehow coaxed into
blooming long after they should have been rotting on the
ground.

Then one evening as I was standing in the drive, searching
the sky for signs of rain, Adam stepped onto his porch,
stretched his arms over his head, took in a big breath then
letting it our slowly. You had to be there to know how
incredibly sexy this whole scene was. He looked over,
caught me smiling in his direction, smiled back. I felt myself
melt into a pool of butter.

That night Adam visited me in my dreams. What an
imagination he has! He came over with a pastry brush,
asked if it was mine.

I'm not sure. "It looks like my brush. It m-m-might be," I
stammer.

"Let's find out," he whispers in my ear then proceeds to brush melted butter all over my naked body. "What fabulous curves he murmurs. What perfect skin."

I am speechless. Covered in butter, beginning to melt in earnest when he sweeps me into his arms and then leaning in close he...snores in my ear. What? Who is snoring? Oh damn. It's my husband, just when my dream was getting good. I try desperately to fall back to sleep, summoning Adam with all my will. He's gone, vanished, snored away by my unsuspecting husband.

The next day, back in real life I see Madge, who I now despise beyond words, leaving for what might be a week-end away. Her matching roll-on and overnight bag are propped next to her as she waits for a taxi. I duck behind my curtains, count to 100 very slowly, then go next door and ring the bell.

Adam answers. He smiles. I melt. I can't think what to say so I stand there like an idiot hoping he will save me from total mortification. In my desperation I am considering asking for a cup of sugar when he speaks:

"I had a dream about you last night, Mrs. Jacobs. It was funny, you were sopping up melted butter from the driveway, using pancakes. I joined you and we had quite a feast."

"And I had a dream about you," I counter, as I step boldly into his house. "Let me tell you all about it, better yet, we can re-enact it. I'm sure you have butter, I just happen to have a pastry brush in here in my apron pocket."

Spare Room   prompt: Home

In my misguided youth, I thought the song was, "Ho-mo on the Range." My kindergarten teacher corrected me. "It's "Home, home on the range," which I found equally confusing. Mom cooked our meals on the range. I pictured tiny buffalo and deer roaming on her flaming stovetop, not a pretty picture.

Growing up, home was not a safe place. I preferred school or my neighbor's house or Grandma Julie's even though it smelled of old vitamin B capsules. I even preferred Grandma Nell's, in spite of her providing only one large bowl of food per visit. The bowl might be Jello or spaghetti or mac and cheese, or baked beans.

"Kids, this will last all weekend. Whenever you're hungry, just dig in."

Ozzie and Harriet had a home where a kid could feel safe. When I learned they were a real family I thought of writing them, asking if they had a spare room. Ozzie didn't work and never yelled. Harriet's hair was never messed up. The boys only got in little bits of trouble that were always resolved in twenty minutes or less.

Harriet: "Boys, this is your new sister. Isn't she cute! Her name is Sandy Rosen. She's Jewish, but we don't mention that word on TV. Other than that, she is just like us. See how neat her hair is? She seems very polite, oh gosh, she might get into mischief. David, you keep an eye on her."

Boys (in unison): "Gee. Swell."

At home with the Nelsons. I could get used to that. Maybe Beaver Cleaver (what an odd choice of names) would live next door with Ward and June. We could picnic together in the park, if Ozzie was willing to leave the house.

Waiting for a letter back from the Nelsons, in an effort to protect myself, I imagined a giant statue holding a light bulb over my head blasting away the darkness. I thought of her when we sang the national anthem, *Goddess America*, especially my favorite verse, "Stand beside her and guide her through the night with a light from a bulb."

Blue Eyes   prompt: Remember

I remember, I remember, wait, don't tell me. I remember.

Ah shit. I forget.

I seem to recall something about a guy in blue: blue jeans, blue chambray shirt, blue eyes. A cute guy at one time, but now an old guy, his white hair tinged with blue in this light. I seem to recall he was right here in this room moments ago.

Or was it my imagination?

Wait! It's coming back to me. He *was* here. He took my blood pressure. No, he took my temperature. Or was it my wallet? I'll just check my purse. Where the hell is my purse? Ah, here we go. My wallet is missing! Just as I suspected. He stole my money.

No, it wasn't that. He stole my heart. Yes indeed. Stole my heart and my dreams and left me here feeling bereft. I love him and come to think of it, he once loved me, too.

Was he my boyfriend? No, more than that. He was my husband. Roger. My husband for decades. No wonder he looks so old. How did I end up with such an ancient guy for a husband? Could it be that I'm old, too? I'll just check my mirror. It's here in my purse, somewhere. Oh, here's my wallet after all. And is this my mirror? Oh! I'm not old. I'm a beautiful twenty-something.

Hold on, this is a photo? Now I remember that guy, that Roger. He's my father. That's it. My good old Dad. And he was just here. No where's he gone off to? Roger? Dad?

Hello? Any one there?

Oh, there you are. Dad? Not my Dad you say? Not my husband? Well, I didn't think so. And could you be a friend? No? OK, fine.

Yes, of course, you can take my blood pressure. I like your eyes, if it's OK to say so. They match your shirt. Aren't you the handsome one. Those eyes, so blue.

I'll never forget them, I'm sure.

For Science   prompt: Walking

She said she wanted to walk with me. Walk and hold hands, even though we were both women and had just met. I agreed because she said it was for science and seemed sincere.

I've walked hand in hand with my daughter, perhaps with Mother in some bygone era, no other women. Connecting in such a personal way with this woman, who called herself Zenith, was an experiment.

"Our palms hold more energy than any other part of our bodies," she stated, "and when we hold on, palm to palm, we connect on an energetic level. We transmit." My palm felt warm in hers, true, but I didn't buy the bit about transmission.

We made our way along a narrow paved path leading to the beach. I could hear the surf although the ocean was not yet in view. As we crested the hill I saw a crowd dressed in heavy overcoats, scarves and gloves as if it were winter in some northern clime, not a sunny day in California.

We drew closer. I now saw this crowd was more of a mob, menacing, armed with boards, bats, bricks, ready to attack.

"What the hell's happening here?" I turned to my companion, then dropped her hand, heading away from her, from the mob.

"Oh, I'm so sorry," she yelled after my retreating form, "that was *my* memory. It haunts me every time I walk near an ocean. A murder took place, in our village..." Her voice faded with increasing distance. I could no longer make out her words. I turned briefly, saw her standing alone on the beach.

The mob was nowhere to be seen.

Alternative Ending   prompt: Breaking Bad

The tough-looking kid out front could be a gang member.
Hard to tell the way kids dress these days: baggy pants,
hoods up shadowing their faces, everything hanging off them
like they don't give a darn.

I figure this boy is some pissed-off teenager, not from around
here. He's walking right up my front steps. I can now see
how red his face is, but not from anger. He's crying. He looks
to be in his twenties maybe more. His round, red face is all
scrunched up, big tears rolling down, crying hard. Not so
tough after all. Not so menacing.

His knock startles me even though I've been watching his
approach. I peer once more into the peephole. All I see is
one giant bloodshot Cyclops eye. I slide back the latch, turn
the deadbolt, open the door.

My God, Jesse! I haven't seen my nephew for years. Little
Jesse, so much taller now but the same sweet face and
blue-blue eyes. His parents gave up on him ages ago, had
him evicted from his Aunt Ginny's house, but I hold no
grudge against him. He took such good care of Ginny in her
final months and drugs can happen to anyone. What you'll
do once you're hooked, that's just more bad luck.

He steps in, still crying. Jesse knows where everything is in
my house. He spent enough Christmases here, running with
his cousins, crawling up on Pap's big armchair, spilling hot
chocolate, sticky with marshmallows on my holiday rug. He
heads straight for my couch, pushes aside my handmade
pillow-dolls and plunks himself down. Head in hands, he
looks down at the floor and starts up sobbing again.

"What is it, honey? How bad can it be?" He looks over at me. His expression about breaks my heart. Despair isn't a strong enough word, he looks so lost, broken, ready to roll over and die. And I see now his face is beat-up, raw, swollen, his hands, too.

I plunk my big old body down next to him, close, and we sit. Eventually he quiets down. Another long while passes before he looks up, glances around the room. I hope he's comforted by how nothing has changed. I haven't had the strength to do much since Pap died, don't see the point. Finally Jesse looks at me square and lets out a long slow sigh.

"Hot chocolate?" I ask.
"Yeah," Jesse almost smiles, "Thanks."
"This place needs some paint," I offer. "We could fix it up nice, you and me."

Author's note: I know there is no Jesse, but there is. For me the thin membrane between reality and fantasy is quite permeable. I felt bad for Jesse as the TV series *Breaking Bad* ended. Although I knew it was fiction I still needed an alternative, one in which Jesse is saved. Perhaps my fictitious aunt will provide Jesse with another chance to reclaim his life.

When I meet people who share a gruesome childhood story with me I often ask, "Was there an adult who enabled you to live to this day?" and there is always someone, a neighbor, a teacher, a relative, who sees the good in a child and helps them find their way.

Additional Titles Available on Amazon.com from:

Mel C. Thompson Publishing Company,
Parent label of:
Cyborg Productions,
Blue Beetle Press,
Citi-Voice Magazine.

*Nippon by **Jonathan Hayes, MCTP.***

*American Haiku by **Jonathan Hayes, MCTP.***

*Short Shorts by **Nancy Margulies, MCTP.***

*Blackpoint by **Russell Lichter, MCTP.***

*Greenpoint by **Russell Lichter, MCTP.***

*Secrets by **Dawne Ashley, MCTP.***

*Caught and Held by **Nancy Depper, Blue Beetle Press.***

*Living the Zine Life by **Mel C. Thompson, MCTP.***

*The Secret Tome by **Mel C. Thompson, MCTP.***

*Diary of A Suburban Zombie
by **Mel C. Thompson, MCTP.***

*Khrushchev Goes To Disneyland
by **Mel C. Thompson, MCTP.***

*When Publishers Stalked The Earth
by **Mel C. Thompson, MCTP.***

*Nothing Holy: Tales of Zen Buddhist Scoundrels,
by **Mel C. Thompson, MCTP.***

About the Author

Nancy Margulies lives in Montara, California, with her (Animal) husband, Gary. She experienced a number of lives before becoming an author of fiction. She was a psychologist, among the first ever to specialize in working with deaf people; a mural painter, the executive director of a large arts organization, a corporate consultant, a performer of one-woman theatrical shows.

During her years in the the corporate world Margulies developed a visual note-taking system that became very popular and is now in use in many countries. As a result of her skill in creating these visual records she traveled the globe, working with The Dalai Lama, Maori tribes in New Zealand, Aboriginal tribes in Australia, President Clinton and his cabinet, Al Gore and hundreds of corporate and community leaders.

A number of her non-fiction books and instructional videos, including the best-selling *Mapping Inner Space*, are available on Amazon. Margulies' first work of fiction, a collection of very short stories, was published by Mel C. Thompson in 2013. Entitled *Short Shorts: Sudden Fiction*, the book received critical acclaim.

Made in the USA
San Bernardino, CA
20 December 2014